Swimming Upstream, Slowly

Swimming Upstream, Slowly

a novel

Melissa Clark

broadway books • new york

PUBLISHED BY BROADWAY BOOKS

Published in the United States by Broadway Books, an imprint of The Doubleday Broadway Publishing Group, a division of Random House, Inc., New York.
www.broadwaybooks.com

Book design by Caroline Cunningham

Library of Congress Cataloging-in-Publication Data

Clark, Melissa, 1949–
Swimming upstream, slowly : a novel / Melissa Clark.— 1st ed.
p. cm.
1. Women television personalities—Fiction. 2. Los Angeles (Calif.)—Fiction. I. Title.

PS3603.L3655S95 2006
813'.6—dc22 2006042607

ISBN-13: 978-0-7679-2526-6
ISBN-10: 0-7679-2526-2

PRINTED IN THE UNITED STATES OF AMERICA

10 9 8 7 6 5 4 3 2 1

First Edition

For my parents,

Ron and Sheila Clark.

Come to think of it,

we never did have that talk about

the birds and the bees.

The child is in me still . . . and sometimes not so still.

—MISTER ROGERS

Swimming Upstream, Slowly

February

one

Sasha Salter squeezed between two pregnant women on her way to the bar for her third round of drinks. She was at her best friend's baby shower, and by the looks of it she was one of the few who weren't expecting. As she slipped past, one of the women slid her pedicured foot forward.

"You're Sasha Salter," the woman declared, as though she were introducing Sasha to Sasha.

"Yes," she said, forcing a smile.

The other pregnant woman lit up. "She's practically having her baby as an excuse to watch your show." They both smiled politely.

"That's sweet," Sasha said, eager for another vodka cranberry. She assumed this was a compliment, but the previous drink was fogging her thoughts, and instead of focusing on the compliment she could focus only on the women's bellies, which stuck out like tongues, seemingly mocking her own slender stomach.

"You've really brought quality back to television," one of the women said, as though she were the Quality Television Authority.

"You should be proud of yourself," the other one said in a maternal tone.

Sasha smiled again and cocked her head with what she hoped indicated a grateful modesty. She looked toward the bar. "Well, I'm just gonna . . ."

"Go," one of them said, laughing. "Have one for me, too."

Sasha drummed her fingers on the bar until the bartender noticed. He was staring at a jar of olives but snapped out of it. "If it weren't for you, I'd have nothing to do today," he joked.

"Everyone's pregnant here," she said, looking around for the restroom. When their eyes met, she noticed a deep sympathy. He handed her the drink.

"Your time will come," he said. He seemed sincere.

"Oh," she started. "That's not what I meant."

He continued looking at her with earnestness.

"I just meant . . ." She took a sip. Suddenly she didn't know what she meant or what she was defending or why, exactly, she felt that the bartender felt sorry for her. Her mind had suddenly gone from foggy to cloudy. The third vodka certainly wasn't going to help clear things up.

She watched the party guests. So many women bursting with new life, her best friend Erika in the middle. She was thrilled for Erika, but what was more pressing was her bladder. She finally found the sign for the ladies' room and, once settled on the toilet, her glass resting on the toilet-paper holder, she pulled out her cell phone and made a drunken call to Jordan.

"Where are you?" he asked.

"On the toilet," she said, because that's where she was.

"I know we're close, but that's a little too much information."

"I'm at Erika's baby shower," she said. "I'm drunk."

"I know," he said.

"How?"

"Baby shower, toilet, cell phone. I know you."

"I didn't mean to—"

"I'm not judging."

"What if I said I was too drunk to drive home and if I see another pregnant person I might retch, and that I'd owe you the biggest favor in the world if you came and picked me up?"

"I don't know how I'd react."

"Well, I'm saying it."

Jordan sighed.

"I hear you're annoyed," she said. "You don't have to be so dramatic."

"Where are you?" he said, his voice taking on an avuncular tone.

"The Four Seasons, Doheny. Stat."

"See you in twenty," he said.

Sasha hung up. She thought how funny life was. Here she was, sitting on the toilet, killing time by playing a frantic game of Tetris on her cell phone. She'd certainly be hungover at work the next day. Hopefully, it would be a mellow one.

She flushed, grabbed her drink, and made her way to the mirror. She was applying mascara when Erika startled her. The wand scratched the bridge of her nose, leaving a black smudge that expanded as she tried to rub it away. "You've been in here for, like, an hour," Erika said.

"I have not," Sasha protested.

"Well, come on." Erika reached for Sasha's arm. "We're about to play the baby-food game."

She's really excited about this, Sasha thought.

"You are *so* the hit of this party," Erika said, her eyes welling up with tears. And then, with a face Sasha could only interpret as prideful, she said, "And you're *my* best friend." Then she touched her stomach. "And his best auntie," she added before leaving the bathroom and heading back to the flock of women in the other room.

~ ~ ~

Blindfolded, Sasha was swirling a melon-flavored gelatinous goo in her mouth when she heard a harsh whisper.

"Sasha!"

"Honeydew," she said through the puree.

A chorus of giggles exploded from the women.

"It's *dates*!" Erika said. "How do you get honeydew from dates?"

Sasha slipped off her blindfold. Jordan was poking his head in the doorway behind her. First one woman looked toward him and then another and another, like meerkats hearing a suspicious noise in the desert. Erika turned, too. "Jordan! Come in!" He looked down at the floor, a sweet, shy gesture, and then gave Sasha an icy, hateful stare.

"That's okay," Sasha said, on Jordan's behalf. "He's my ride. I have to get going."

She hugged Erika, Erika's mom, aunt, and one of the pregnant women before making her exit. She returned a second later to retrieve her purse, which was spattered with baby food.

"Sometimes I think you put me in these situations to make it look like you have a boyfriend," Jordan said as he drove down Doheny.

Her normal response would be a curt "Fuck you," but ever since the show Sasha had been trying to curb her potty mouth.

"Who can you call if not your best friend?" she said instead. "I'd do it for you."

At a red light Sasha turned to the car next to her. A little girl was glued to the backseat window, staring. Sasha couldn't tell if the girl recognized her, and she hated to assume she did, but she gave an obligatory wave. The light turned green before she could see the girl's response. As the car drove away, she noticed a KILL YOUR TELEVISION bumper sticker. "Now you're all mad at me," she said, copping a grumpy attitude, though she didn't feel at all grumpy: she felt divine, being chauffeured around.

"I have things to do," Jordan said. "And this wasn't in the plan."

The plan, the plan. He was always talking about the plan, as if order and reason had anything to do with living in this world. She should know—her entire life right now was as arbitrary as it came. Jordan would argue that it was all part of the bigger plan, but it wasn't. It couldn't be. Just two years ago, Sasha had been swimming her way through the murky waters of higher education—soaking up the principles of early-childhood education. Immersed in courses like Creative Dramatics for Primary Grades and The Young Child in the Family and Community. Then suddenly this new life—the accolades, the awards, the power. A select group of people handing her something she knew very little about. They made her executive producer of *Please Pass the Salter,* her weekly program on the Public Broadcasting channel. She was referred to as "Miss Rogers with sass," and the *Wall Street Journal* wrote, "Who needs the Wiggles when you've got the giggles?"

Her master's degree had revolved around humor and childhood, and instead of writing the same dull 120-page thesis she created a world for kids that combined learning and laughter—a *Saturday Night Live* format, only smarter and funnier and for Saturday mornings. She wasn't the first to explore this arena—*Zoom*, *The Electric Company*, *Sesame Street* had all paved the way for her—but her goal was to make humor the constant, because, once instilled in children, she believed it was the most important coping skill they could receive in life.

And then, as if to say, "You think *that's* funny," a crazy set of circumstances unraveled. Her professor met a producer at a dinner party for the dean of the university. The producer, an alumnus of the school, had gone on to produce a string of "end-of-the-world" movie hits and, since becoming a father, wanted to change direction in his career—do something to make his kid proud. He was searching for a quality children's vehicle. That's what he called it: *vehicle*. The professor, a champion of Sasha from the moment he'd read her graduate-school application, and then later, surreptitiously, a lover, announced the name of his prized student: Sasha Salter. The producer said, so the story goes, "Sasha Salter sounds like the name of a person who's going places." And then, "I should know—that's what I told Halle Berry."

And so X led to Y led to Z, which led to Sasha in the car with her best friend Jordan, going somewhere, as the producer had said, but where she wasn't quite sure. "What about my car?" she suddenly realized.

"We're going to get you caffeinated and then get you back to your car."

The man with a plan. Sasha lifted the armrest between them and snuggled in close.

"I'm not the boyfriend," he cautioned her, but she didn't mind. His arm felt cool against her warm head.

"I'm not asking for your hand in marriage," she said. "I'm just asking for a place to lean." He didn't move his arm, and she stayed in that position until they reached their destination.

two

At work the next day, Sasha was greeted by a mousy girl with glasses. She was covering a story for a popular women's magazine, "20 Under 30—Ones to Watch." When Sasha first heard that she'd been selected to be featured, along with a young woman working with malaria patients in Vietnam and an advocate for elephants, among others, she called her parents. It was just one more in a series of calls starting with "Mom, they're turning my thesis into a TV show" and continuing with "Dad, I'm moving to Los Angeles, they want me in the show, we were nominated for a Daytime Emmy, we won the Daytime Emmy, grab this week's *People,* listen to NPR. . . ." The calls just kept coming, like a spray of happy bullets.

Her dad, a college engineering professor, and her mom, a high-school history teacher, were thrilled for her, but she wouldn't say that they relished her success. In fact, she wasn't even sure they considered it success. Her mom once asked if she still planned to go on for her Ph.D. "when this is through." Sasha didn't think in terms of the future anymore. She was firmly rooted in the present, and it felt right.

Everyone was on-set, rehearsing a scene for taping later that day. This was Sasha's favorite segment of the show, "Mixed-Up Tairy Fales." It was one of the ideas that had made it from the thesis to the show. Today's sketch was "Big Red Riding Hood," and Sasha herself was playing Big Red, fat suit and all. Fritz, a regular cast member, was playing the Wolf, not the Big Bad Wolf but the Little Nice Wolf. The camera was able to shrink him in size, and a computer-generated halo was placed over his head. Instead of skipping off to Grandma's house, Big Red walked at a snail's pace. The visiting journalist took copious notes. What could she possibly be writing? The director asked Sasha to waddle more—to really feel the weight of Big Red. Sasha loved the director's seriousness, as if he were Milos Forman or Roman Polanski.

~ ~ ~

Melanie, the journalist, was fresh out of college. She wore tan cat-shaped glasses that added pep to her strangely boring face. She had a tangle of wiry brown hair that desperately needed *something*—a cut, a shape, some conditioner. Despite her appearance, Sasha liked her company. Together, after the taping of the Big Red segment, they sat in her dressing room eating strawberries.

"These are *amaaaazing,*" Melanie said, examining one. "They're so huge!"

"You're not from California, are you?" Sasha said, kicking back on the musty green couch.

"Ohio," she replied. "These are, like, quintessential strawberries." She finally put the thing into her mouth. Her eyes rolled back in ecstasy. Sasha wondered if she'd ever had an orgasm. Could strawberries really cause so much pleasure?

"I'm from Boston," Sasha said, and suddenly Melanie snapped out of her strawberry reverie and scribbled some notes in her book.

"So, did you get assigned to me? Or did you pick this story? Or what?" Sasha asked, sincerely curious.

"Oh, I pitched you," Melanie answered.

"Really," Sasha said.

"The magazine's trying to go hip." She snorted. "Next month you'll see an article on the Venice boardwalk. That's what they consider hip. Maybe that was hip thirty years ago, but quite frankly I call that place tourist hell, ya know?"

Sasha nodded in agreement, though she'd been there only once, biking on a bad blind date. She noticed her appointment book on the end table and picked it up as Melanie continued.

"So I said, 'You want hip? I'll give you hip.' I told them to watch your show that Saturday and we'd discuss my pitch on Monday. So Monday comes around and we gather in the conference room and they go, 'Save your breath, just get her interview.' "

Sasha loved the story, but at the same time she realized that she had a gynecologist appointment later that afternoon. She must have made a disappointed face, because Melanie said, "I know, I didn't really pitch *you,* but I did pitch your show."

"That's awesome," Sasha said. "I love that." She closed her date book and took another strawberry. "So how does this work?" she asked. "Do you ask me a bunch of questions and I have to give you thoughtful, witty answers?"

"I was hoping I could just shadow you for about a week, and I could get to know your life through your days, y'know?"

Sasha remembered her own journalistic endeavors in college. In Journalism 101 she'd had to conduct an interview with a working professional. While other students chose professors or administrators or parents, Sasha picked up the phone book and called a local psychic. The older, suspicious-looking man showed up for their appointment in her dorm's common area, and after he answered her barrage of sophomoric questions (How long have you been a psychic? Do you like your job? What was the worst experience, the best?) he offered to read her and she agreed. She picked a few cards from his tarot deck, and he proceeded to tell her that one of her past lives included working as a maid at the Isabella Stewart Gardner Museum in Boston, and another included constructing the Golden Gate Bridge. He said it with such certainty that she had to believe him. She got only a B on her paper, but suddenly everyone in the dorm knew her as the girl with the past lives—which added a certain panache to her reputation.

"You mean follow me around at work?" Sasha asked.

"Work and home, if that's okay."

Sasha thought about her quiet life outside of work—a stack of novels she wanted to get through, her bare living room that she wanted to paint a vivid red, dinner with friends. Why would anyone want to read about that? "You don't want to shadow me to a doctor's appointment, do you?" she asked.

"I'm so there."

~ ~ ~

The waiting room was empty, but Dr. Banks was running late, so Sasha and Melanie chatted, surrounded by baby pictures and parenting magazines. "You can put in your article 'Sasha Salter believes in the power of the Pap smear,' " she joked. Melanie squirmed. "She's a really good doctor," Sasha went on, "in case you're looking." Melanie was silent, and Sasha suddenly knew for a fact that she was indeed a virgin.

"Do you consider yourself an advocate for children?" Melanie asked, changing the subject.

"An advocate for children . . ." Sasha took a hard look into herself for the answer. "Yes, I guess, but more than that I think lately I'm an advocate for good television."

Melanie touched her pen to her chin. "But your background is in education, so wouldn't your first priority be children and education?"

Sasha wanted to answer, she did, but all of a sudden the door opened and the nurse looked at Melanie.

"Sasha?"

Melanie pointed.

"I'll see ya in a few," Sasha said as she headed to the bathroom to pee in a cup.

Dr. Banks was a slight woman with a generous smile and a kind disposition. It was clear that she would end up in a helping profession, Sasha thought.

"My kids absolutely adore your show," she said, preparing her torture instruments.

"Thank you so much."

"Was it on when I last saw you?"

"No, I think we were only in pre-production," Sasha said, flinging the term around like a pro.

"When I first saw it I was so excited. 'That's my patient! That's my patient!' I said it to my kids, not to anyone else."

Sasha smiled. Everyone loved to claim knowing her now that she was on television. Even the mailman once said he was honored to deliver her mail. She could only imagine what it was like to be a real celebrity.

"Why don't you scootch down on the table," Dr. Banks suggested.

Sasha complied, and as soon as she felt the hard metal she employed the visualization and breathing techniques her director had taught her before her first taping. *She's lying on the beach, a gentle wind blows. The ebb and flow of the water. A hard metal appliance scraping her cervix. The smell of salt air.*

"Relax," Dr. Banks said. "I'm almost done."

Hot sun beating down, the softness of the sand.

"Ow, ow, ow . . ." She emitted these sounds as Dr. Banks pulled the instrument out.

"No one likes this," Dr. Banks said. "I'd worry if they did."

Sasha breathed a sigh of relief. She wouldn't have to go through this for another whole year.

"What are your kids' names? I can send them an autograph or something," Sasha offered. Nervous chatter.

"Oh, isn't that sweet," Dr. Banks said. "Ethan and Mia. They'd be thrilled. Go ahead and get dressed, I'll be right back."

Dr. Banks left the room, and Sasha ripped off her paper gown. She slid from the examination table and looked back at the metal stirrups her feet were just in. The power of the Pap smear, she thought. A degrading act, but imperative nonetheless. She put on her blue bra and white underwear, and caught a glimpse of herself in the mirror—why was there a mirror in the changing area? She ran her fingers through her brown hair. It felt silky against her hand. She smiled at herself, a closed-mouth grin, and then she widened it, her mouth slightly ajar. What if it was a two-way mirror and Dr. Banks was on the other side, watching? Sasha had one foot in her skirt when there was a knock on her door and a bewildered-looking Dr. Banks entered before she could say that she wasn't yet dressed. For an instant, Sasha thought Dr. Banks had actually seen her.

Sasha quickly stuck her other leg into her skirt, feeling modest, even though the doctor had just seen her insides. She stood up straight in her bra and skirt. "Is everything okay?" She had a quick flush of worry.

Dr. Banks looked at her quizzically. "I just did a routine check of your urine sample." And then, "You're pregnant."

Sasha thought she heard her doctor say she was pregnant. She shook her head. "Wait, what?"

"Sasha, you're pregnant. You look a little stunned, so I don't know whether to congratulate you."

Sasha was suddenly back in fifth grade. Mrs. Singer was at the chalkboard drawing a flowchart of a boy's penis going into a girl's vagina, the result being a tiny baby. Sasha was as shocked now as she was then. She stumbled back to the examination table and sat down between the stirrups.

"It's absolutely impossible," she said, feeling light-headed. Was this a dream?

Dr. Banks looked at her sweetly but sadly. "This was unexpected," she said, with a doctor's wisdom and absence of judgment.

Sasha had not had sex in more than two years. She scanned her memory for traces of recent intercourse but came up empty. She and Jordan were always joking about how long it had been for both of them—Jordan finally giving in last month to a fling with his dental hygienist. Sasha was pissed that he'd beaten her to the punch and pretended to get mad at the hygienist. "How is she ever going to clean your teeth again?" No, it was certain: Sasha hadn't had sex in two years. The last time was with Sean, and before that Blake, and before that with her professor, and before that . . .

She spoke in a calm and calculated manner, as though she were explaining an errant phone bill to a customer-service representative. "I have not had sex in over two years," she said.

Dr. Banks sat down on her stool and put her hand on Sasha's knee.

"This is absolutely impossible," Sasha repeated. She suddenly thought about the three vodka cranberries she'd downed the day before at Erika's baby shower. Maybe being around all those pregnant women had tricked her own body into thinking it was pregnant. She knew it happened with menstruation, why not with pregnancy?

"I was at a baby shower," she stammered. "Just yesterday."

Dr. Banks smiled. "It's not contagious."

Suddenly Sasha realized that she had indeed skipped her last period. Her body was prone to do that under duress; it wasn't abnormal for her. "I didn't get my period last month," she told the doctor.

"That's because you're pregnant."

"I don't even have a boyfriend!" Sasha countered. She was moving from a growing anxiety into a full-blown panic. She hosted a children's program, she worked fourteen-hour days. She couldn't even get a dog for this reason; she could barely sustain plant life. Babies were something to contemplate far in her future, not now, not during the most exciting time of her life. She pictured Melanie outside in the waiting room, legs crossed, thumbing through an old issue of *Parenting*.

Dr. Banks stood up. Sasha detected frustration. But it was she who was frustrated. "Couldn't this all be some big mistake?" she asked, hot tears streaming down her face. She loved her job. She loved where she was in her life now. This complication made no sense. "I mean, you can't get pregnant without a guy. Maybe you got someone else's urine sample."

Dr. Banks put her hand on Sasha's shoulder. "Here's what I want you to do. I want you to go home, get a good night's sleep, come back here tomorrow morning, and we're going to start from scratch."

"You want me to just go home?"

"I think it's best at this point. Fresh day tomorrow, right?"

Sasha knew that the doctor wanted her to come back with news: "Oh, my God! I totally forgot I slept with fill-in-the-blank last month! Silly me!"

Dr. Banks tucked some papers into Sasha's chart and picked it up. "We'll deal with billing tomorrow," she said. "You just go home now."

Sasha almost walked out in her bra, but then suddenly saw her shirt resting sloppily on the chair. She picked it up, threw it over her head, wiped her face, and followed Dr. Banks into the hallway. She could see Melanie through the sliding window. Indeed, her legs were crossed, and she was thumbing through a magazine.

"Tomorrow at eight-thirty?" Dr. Banks asked.

Sasha walked zombielike into the waiting room. Melanie looked up. "Hey! Did you know it's recommended that kids don't watch any TV before the age of two?" She put the magazine down and stood up, following Sasha out the door. "I'd love to find out your thoughts on that," she said, seemingly unfazed by Sasha's state of shock.

three

After the doctor's, Melanie suggested that they have dinner together before meeting again the next morning. Sasha tried to soften her icy tone, but she had to make it clear that dinner was impossible. "Not tonight, Melanie," she said. Whenever her mother was mad, she used Sasha's name to emphasize her anger. Now Sasha was doing the same.

"Well, how about a drink?" Melanie persisted.

A drink? No, she couldn't have a drink. "I can't," she said, and then added, "I have to deal with a personal situation tonight."

"Did something happen at the doctor's?" Melanie asked.

All these questions were what had probably landed Melanie in this profession in the first place. Sasha tried to figure out a convincing way to answer her. A strong dislike was bubbling up inside her for this once enjoyable sidekick.

"No, no, no," she said, adding a convincing giggle. "It's not that, it's just . . ." She searched for a word but couldn't find it.

"So where's your car?" she asked instead. They climbed into Sasha's new Saab. "I'll drive you there, and then I have to go."

"It's at the set," Melanie said. "Where did you think it was?"

Sasha didn't answer. She wanted Melanie to stop talking, to stop asking questions. In fact, she was at the point now where if Melanie opened her mouth and any sound whatsoever came out, she would slam on the brakes and politely ask her to leave. Thankfully, they sat in silence during the fifteen-minute drive back to work.

~ ~ ~

Sasha was six when Ben Turner had cornered her in the class coat closet and put one hand on her chest and mashed his lips into her cheek.

"What are you doing?" she'd screamed, wriggling out of his grasp.

"That's how people have babies," he said.

"It is not."

Ben was little and nice, and she didn't understand why his actions made her feel so bad.

"I don't want a baby!" Sasha protested.

"Too bad, you're gonna have one now."

Sasha hadn't known the details of babies and how they were made, so she'd worried that Ben was right. She ran out of the closet and told her teacher, who was helping another student tie his shoe. The teacher listened intently to Sasha and then ushered her to her desk, where she kneeled down. "Thank you for telling me," the teacher said. "Whenever something makes you feel bad, you can always tell me."

"What happens when the baby comes?" Sasha asked.

"You don't have to worry," she said. "Kids can't have babies. Only grown-ups." And then she went to find Ben.

Now Sasha felt like her six-year-old self all over again—scared, angry, confused. She yearned for someone—anyone—to kneel down beside her and tell her this was all just a silly mistake, that she didn't have to worry.

Once home, she collapsed on the bed with her cordless phone and immediately dialed Jordan. He picked up after one ring. He sounded bothered.

"Hel—"

"It's me," Sasha said. "I need you to come over here, more than I've ever needed you to come over in the past."

"Can I call you back?"

No, he couldn't, and just the thought of him hanging up made her burst into tears.

"Are you okay?" he asked, still bothered, but now slightly concerned.

"Please, please, please come over. I don't care when, just say you'll come over," she cried.

"Did someone die?" he asked.

"No," she assured him. "No, not that. But I need you." She emphasized the word *need* so that he would get the severity. Then she hung up the phone and sat back to wait.

~ ~ ~

"I thought you said you hadn't had sex since Sean," Jordan said when she told him she was apparently pregnant.

"I haven't," Sasha said.

"Don't bullshit me," Jordan said.

"I'm not."

"But it's impossible."

Sasha was in bed, and Jordan was sitting up next to her. He kept handing her tissues. She was starting to feel tired, and not just regular sleepy-tired but drained-tired, limbs-heavy tired. She didn't feel much like talking. "*Rrnnrr,*" she grunted.

"You'll know more tomorrow," Jordan said. "I mean, what can we really do till then?" She liked the way he'd inserted himself into her problem. Then again, she couldn't believe she had a potential problem in the first place.

Jordan finally admitted that he had a date later that night. Not with the dental hygienist but with a writer. He'd met her on a Jewish dating site, though neither he nor she was Jewish. Sasha laughed. "Sounds perfect," she said. "What's her name?"

"Echo."

"Echo? Only *you* would meet a girl named Echo."

He'd been on the other line with her when Sasha called him earlier. Echo was having second thoughts, and he was doing everything to convince her to meet him that night.

Sasha rolled over onto her side. "Even if I'm not pregnant . . ."

"Which you're not," Jordan said.

"It's just so weird that this is happening."

"Agreed," Jordan said. "And maybe you'll switch doctors when all is said and done."

"But I like her."

Just then the phone rang. Jordan was holding it, because he'd called to check his own messages earlier, and impulsively, unfortunately, he picked up. "Sasha's phone." Sasha shot him a look. He shrugged an apology.

"Oh, hi, Mrs. Salter." Sasha dived under the covers. "I'm fine, thank you." Jordan's formality sounded insincere. "Yes, she is, let me get her." He pressed his hand over the mouthpiece and called out as though Sasha were on the other side of the apartment. She emerged from the blankets and grabbed the phone from him, scratching him with her nail by mistake. "I'm bleeding!" he said incredulously, and stood up to wash off the trickle of blood in the bathroom.

"Hi, Mom!" she said, mustering up some strength from deep within. "I'm great, how are you?"

From the bathroom came the sound of water running and Jordan muttering something about Jesus Christ.

"How's Dad? Good. Work's great! Yeah, everything's great."

Jordan emerged from the bathroom holding his finger and shaking his head. Now she shrugged in a halfhearted apology—to herself? Her parents? Jordan? She motioned for him to come closer, and he did. He extended his hand to show his wound. She listened to her mother as she pressed her lips to his finger.

four

Sasha was sitting in Dr. Banks's office. Next to her was a large framed portrait of the doctor's kids, Mia and Ethan. She was still crying. The second urine test and then the blood test had come back positive. Dr. Banks now looked concerned. Sasha swore over and over that she had not been sexually active in more than two years. How could she? The show took up all of her time. She wasn't even attracted to anyone on-set, let alone sleeping with anyone. Sasha felt like she was back in high school, pleading with her ethics teacher to believe that she hadn't plagiarized her ethics paper—her ethics paper, of all things! She might not have been an A student, but she was smart enough to be ethical in ethics.

Dr. Banks let out a sigh. "I'm not going to lie to you," she said. "This is troubling."

"Tell me about it!" Sasha said. "Please, this is more than troubling."

Dr. Banks tried one more route. "Is it possible that you were at a bar where someone might have gotten hold of—"

"I don't go to bars," Sasha said. "I work. It's all I do. I don't have a social life right now. I can't even remember the last time I went out on a weekend. No one slipped me a roofie, or whatever that drug is called."

"Rohypnol," the doctor said. She rested a pencil against her chin. "Okay, there's someone I know . . ." and then she stopped.

Sasha waited for her to continue, but instead Dr. Banks tapped the eraser against her chin. Silence persisted. Sasha looked around Dr. Banks's office. In addition to the framed pictures of her kids, there were framed degrees—B.S. from Yale, M.D. from Stanford. Sasha's degrees were shoved in a drawer somewhere. She wondered if she should frame and hang them, too.

"He's doing some interesting work at UCLA," she finally said. She exchanged the pencil for a pen and scribbled something on a piece of paper. "He's not actually practicing at UCLA, but the university is funding him, in a circuitous way." Sasha was confused. "I think I want you to see him before we discuss anything else. Like termination . . . or not."

"Or not?" Sasha said. "If this is true, I have no other choice but to terminate." She couldn't help it, but the word conjured up Arnold Schwarzenegger. Her head was spinning. It was now nine-twenty, and Sasha had to zoom over to work and what? Pretend everything was fine? Put on her fat suit and waddle down the stage toward the Little Nice Wolf?

"You know what I'd like you to do?" Dr. Banks said, perking up. "Make a list of your sexual partners—all of them—since you became sexually active."

Sasha's mind went to work: glimpses of herself naked

flashed through her memory. Did "sexually active" mean actual intercourse? What about just kissing? Touching? She had to find out. "By sexual partners, do you mean people I've had sex with?" she asked.

Dr. Banks looked up at her over her glasses. She put her pen down and spoke in a serious manner. "Yes, your sexual partners are people you've had sexual intercourse with. Penetration."

Sasha felt like a shamed schoolgirl. "So, no one I've just kissed or anything."

Was she imagining it, or did Dr. Banks look annoyed? "Start with actual lovers," she said. "Let's start there."

Sasha sighed and brought a tissue to her eyes and wiped away an errant tear. She'd stopped crying, but her face was wet with streaks. Dr. Banks stood up and handed her a piece of paper. "By the time you call him, I will have spoken to him."

Sasha took the paper.

"He'll call me after you see him. We'll go from there."

Sasha tried to pull herself together. She smoothed out her pants, which had become wrinkled from sitting. She had a final concern, so she voiced it. "This is all confidential, right?" she said.

Dr. Banks's calm, sympathetic look reappeared. "Sasha, of course."

"I'm no Julia Roberts, but I just don't want anybody knowing about this. I mean, besides you and Dr.—" She looked at the piece of paper and tried to make out the writing. "Richm—"

"Rusmeuth," Dr. Banks said. "No one but us," she confirmed. "You have enough on your plate. Don't worry about that."

Sasha smiled, relieved, if only for an instant.

~ ~ ~

When Sasha walked into work, numb and confused, Melanie was sitting outside her dressing room talking on her cell phone. "Oh, she's finally here," she said. "I'll talk to you later."

"Hi, hi," Sasha said, annoyed but hiding it. Melanie looked at her watch, but Sasha ignored the gesture. Instead, she unlocked the door and the two entered.

"I just wrote up a bunch of questions last night. I was hoping I could grab you for, like, half an hour, since we lost time last night and this morning."

Sasha put her bag down on the couch and checked the daily schedule posted on the mirror. There was a writers' session at ten, which she didn't run but always sat in on in full participation. Lunch was at twelve, and then they had a few musical numbers to rehearse with the band before taping on Friday.

"Today's tough," she said, still looking at the schedule, though she had absorbed all the information it had to give. She glanced up at Melanie, who had a hand on her hip. If there had been a thought bubble over her head, it would have read, "You're pissing me off." Melanie joined her in front of the schedule.

"Well, what about lunch?"

Sasha hesitated, then said, "I can't. Doctor's appointment." She tried to pass it off as insignificant as an oil change, so she added, "Nothing to do with yesterday's appointment, so don't go worrying."

Sasha looked at herself in the mirror. She didn't look right. Her eyes were puffy from crying, and her hair was flat and pressed against her head. Something about her chin looked out of place. She normally had a hard, strong chin, but now, upon closer inspection, she noticed that it had gone soft. And then it hit her. She was pregnant. She sucked in her cheeks, then released them.

"Who's worried?" Melanie said, taking a seat on Sasha's green couch. "I'm just trying to do my job."

~ ~ ~

Sasha loved being in the writers' room. The writers were the heartbeat of the show, and she felt they were the only department that was as passionate about it as she was. Ross, one of the writers, had once called her at home to tell her that he'd literally dreamed a segment, and later they were even able to use it. She was envious that he had absorbed the show into his unconscious, but more than that she was delighted, euphoric even. These eight men and women—most of them older, smarter, and funnier than she—were all here because of a creative thesis. Not a day went by that she didn't marvel at that.

Sasha was sitting at the head of the table, next to Pam Newall, the head writer, when her cell phone rang. She instinctively picked it up. Jordan was on the other end. "How'd it go?" he asked. "I've been waiting for your call."

Sasha pressed the phone hard into her ear. She looked up at the group. No one seemed to be listening. They were bouncing Jelly Bellies off the table and into cups.

"Yeah!" Sasha said, trying to sound extra enthusiastic. "Right! It's true!"

At the other end of the table, Ross opened his mouth and Michael tossed a jelly bean his way. Ross caught it, and the other writers exploded in applause. Ross swallowed and then opened his mouth to accept more.

"It's true?" Jordan asked. "You're sure?"

Now jelly beans were flying everywhere, and Ross, who had suddenly become all mouth, was out of his chair and trying to catch them. Melanie sat in the corner, an eyebrow arched, taking in the scene.

"Yeah, how about I call you at lunch?" Sasha said. "I'll call you on my way to my appointment."

"Oh, so you don't know for sure," Jordan said, relieved.

"Call ya in a bit," Sasha said, suddenly irritated at everything: Jordan's relief, the flying Jelly Bellies—green, yellow, purple—sailing through the air, Melanie's scowl, the article in general. Sasha put the phone on the table and cleared her throat. "So are we working today or what?" she asked, a little snide, uncharacteristic. Ross and Michael and Pam and everyone else heard her—really heard her—and settled down like reluctant schoolchildren.

Pam stood up by the chart they had developed. "Any way we can incorporate jelly beans into a sketch?" she asked. Everybody went to work, trying to figure it out.

five

Dr. Rusmeuth's office was on the fringe of Westwood—the area around UCLA—upstairs from a local sporting-goods store. Sasha climbed the stairs, heart pounding and feeling, again, on the verge of tears. She was surprised to see a typical doctor's office waiting room—magazines on tables, office furniture, and that inexplicable waiting-room smell. It was empty, and Sasha was relieved. The woman at the front desk slid her window open.

"Sasha?" she asked.

"Yes?"

"Dr. Rusmeuth is running a few minutes late, but he certainly is expecting you."

Sasha didn't appreciate the front-desk lady knowing anything about her, but she seemed to. She handed Sasha a clipboard with a flurry of papers on it. "Everything's two-sided," she said, referring to the paperwork, but Sasha thought, at that moment, she was referring to her situation.

Her cell phone rang as she answered questions about her sexual health (was her lack of sexual activity considered unhealthy? she wondered). She noticed it was work, so she answered. It was one of her producers, Sarah. The band never received the sheet music, so they were switching the schedule.

The window slid open and the lady behind the desk shot her a look of disappointment and pointed to a sign that Sasha hadn't noticed before: ABSOLUTELY NO CELL PHONES. Sasha returned a look of sincere apology while Sarah rambled on about a flaky production assistant and his unreliable car. She hung up without saying goodbye. The woman behind the desk slid her window shut before Sasha could apologize.

~ ~ ~

She thought she had it under control, but as soon as they started talking her fear, worry, and concern bubbled to the surface and spilled over in tears. She wiped them away, but they continued to flow.

"I'm really freaked out," she said. "This doesn't make sense."

Dr. Rusmeuth didn't seem to notice the tears. He was busy reading her chart. He seemed anxious, excited.

"I must tell you, I was very intrigued by Dr. Banks's call." He looked up at Sasha and softened when he saw her tear-stained face. "We'll figure this out," he said, reassuring her.

Dr. Rusmeuth was peppered with freckles and much younger than she had anticipated—early forties, she guessed. He wore a plain gold wedding band. He was not attractive, and she wondered what the beginning of his courtship had been like—what his wife saw in him that kept her coming back for more. His eyes darted back and forth behind his glasses as he read and reread her paperwork. Her charts from Dr. Banks were on curled fax paper before him.

"I'll tell you the known," he said, confident, sure. Maybe that's what Mrs. Rusmeuth saw. "You *are* pregnant."

Every time she heard the word it felt like a stab in the neck. Muscles were doing all sorts of strange things in her body as of late, tightening and pinching.

"And now for the unknown." He took a dramatic pause. "How?"

Sasha wasn't in the mood for theatrics. "This isn't possible," she said, as though saying it over and over would make it go away. "How can this be happening?"

Dr. Rusmeuth sat back in his chair. "I specialize in men's fertility," he said. "It's something I'm passionate about. Something very close to my heart." Why was he telling her this? She pictured Mrs. Rusmeuth, alone and childless at home. "There's a medical term I helped establish, *Lazicum spermatozoa,* which translates as 'lazy sperm.' " Sasha pictured an animated sperm, a joint dangling out of its mouth, a Keanu Reeves expression on its face. The doctor kept talking, but she was having trouble following. Two doctors had now confirmed that she was pregnant. She wondered if this was how the Virgin Mary had felt—astounded, ashamed, apprehensive.

There were lots of Latin terms being thrown around and then something about the mainstream medical community not embracing his work—and his *determination*. He used the word over and over.

"Has this happened to anyone else?" Sasha asked when he was done with his soliloquy. She meant aside from Mary.

He paused and drummed his fingers on his desk. "There have been some rare situations in the ballpark of this field, yes.

But personally I've never seen a patient who has presented like this."

"Well, is there someone you can put me in touch with? Another patient I can talk to?" Sasha asked.

Rusmeuth shook his head. "We've got very strict confidentiality rules," he said. "Researchers are talking, but I'm afraid we can't divulge patient information."

She didn't understand. What did he mean there were "rare situations in the ballpark of this field"? What field? The lazy-sperm field?

"We've seen elements of this in nature," Dr. Rusmeuth said. "Which is how we originally hypothesized that this could happen to humans. For example, *Lasiurus cinereus*."

Sasha looked at him blankly.

"The hoary bat," he said, clarifying.

This made her feel worse. "Whorey bat?" Sasha asked. "Whore as in *whore*?"

Rusmeuth wrote something on a piece of paper. She looked at it. H-O-A-R-Y.

"Mating occurs in early autumn. The female bat will store the male sperm inside her over the winter, and then in the spring, when she's ready to ovulate, the egg will become fertilized."

It was then that Sasha noticed the wall behind Rusmeuth: a giant framed poster, like a family tree, of the order Chiroptera—bats. It branched out into two subcategories—Megachiroptera and Microchiroptera—and below those sprouted more branches and more names. Sasha caught a glimpse of the hoary bat, *Lasiurus cinereus*, and quickly turned away. Was she merely a step, a hiccup, a burp in the evolutionary process? Why hadn't Dr. Banks warned her that she was being sent to see Bat Man?

Dr. Rusmeuth turned his attention to his computer. He punched a few keys and swiveled the screen so that Sasha could see it. The computer blinked to life, exposing an animated view of a woman's lower half, abdomen and legs. "I want to illustrate what I think is going on here," he said. He moved the arrow to the midsection and clicked; suddenly ovaries and a Fallopian tube appeared. He moved his finger to the figure's vagina.

"When a sperm enters the canal, it swims upstream," he said. "Millions are released in a single ejaculation. Most of them die before ever reaching an egg. When one does reach and penetrate an egg—voilà! Conception. It never fails to astound me," he added.

Sasha looked down at her lap and then back at the image on the screen. "But this clearly isn't what happened in my case," she said.

"Sperm are very fragile little fellows," he continued, "and getting more so every day. Things you wouldn't expect affect them. For example, cell phones, laptop computers, even car-seat warmers. The little buggers can mutate, become inactive, more active. They can do things we don't even know about yet. I like to call them the tricksters."

"What about for me?" Sasha asked again.

"When we talk about sperm's ability to travel, we're talking about sperm *motility,*" Rusmeuth said.

Okay, Sasha thought. *Motility.* Sounds like *mobility.*

"So when we test a man for infertility, we're testing his sperm for motility, among other things. Now, when we talk about the . . . so to speak . . . *handsomeness* of sperm, we're talking about *morphology*."

Sasha wondered if she should be taking notes, if this would turn up as an answer on *Jeopardy!*: "I'll take sperm mutations for a thousand, Alex." If a sperm was handsome, was an egg beautiful? Was the handsome sperm inside so attracted to her beautiful egg that he stuck around, wearing her egg down until she said, "Yes, come in. You win."

Rusmeuth kept talking. He didn't seem to realize that this was a new language for her—that she had to learn individual words before she could comprehend full sentences. "I think what we have here," he finally said, "is a combination of a tenacious sperm mixed with a very hospitable environment." He lifted his fingers off the keyboard. "It's exceedingly rare." His eyes bulged behind his glasses. His excitement was palpable in the way he tapped his foot and twitched his shoulder.

Sasha was beginning to feel very far away, as though she were watching someone else's doctor's appointment.

"Were you able to come up with a list of all your past partners?" Rusmeuth asked. "I know Dr. Banks asked you for that."

Sasha had forgotten, and suddenly she was embarrassed to tell him. It's not like there were *that* many—she wasn't a *whorey* bat. She could probably create the list here, now, in front of Rusmeuth, but she'd rather do it amid the comforts of home, with triggers like yearbooks and journals.

"I've just been so busy at work," she said, her excuse for everything.

"We need to move fast," he said. "You're already eight weeks—"

"Eight weeks!" Sasha crossed her legs. "I'm eight weeks?" she repeated.

"You're going to have decisions to make—keeping the child, perhaps adoption."

"Abortion," Sasha stated flatly, adding to his list. No matter what the circumstances, it seemed obvious to her that a baby just didn't fit into the picture right now.

He wagged a finger at her. "I know this is a sensitive time for you, but if my theory stands this is an enormous medical discovery."

Was he pressuring her? The room was disjointed and suddenly there were two Dr. Rusmeuths. She looked from one to the other. They were both gazing at her chart. She felt hot, then cold, then hot again.

"I think I might—" She was out before she could finish the sentence.

When she came to, she had been moved to the doctor's couch and both he and the front-desk lady were standing nearby.

"There she is!" the lady announced in a singsong manner, a reassuring smile on her face.

"We're both very overwhelmed," Dr. Rusmeuth explained. "For different reasons, of course."

The lady nodded. "This is certainly big."

Dr. Rusmeuth stood in Sasha's line of vision. "Is there someone we can call to come pick you up?" he asked.

Sasha slowly sat up on her elbows and then hoisted herself upright.

"I can call your parents or your boyfriend," the lady offered.

"I don't have a boyfriend," Sasha said.

The lady reached out her hand for Sasha.

She didn't need her help. "I'm okay," she said, inching up from her seat. "I'm gonna make my list and then . . . and then . . ."

"And then I'd like you to bring it to me tomorrow," Dr. Rusmeuth said. "Same time, if it's good for you. We'll go on from there."

What was with all these doctors sending her home and summoning her back the very next day? Sasha finally stood up. "I don't think I can," she said. "I'm extremely busy at work." She looked at the lady, who was nodding. "I'm sort of *newly* in the public eye," Sasha explained.

"Yes, you host a children's television show," the doctor said. "Dr. Banks told me. I must confess I've never seen it."

"I've heard of it," the lady piped up. "It's very reputable."

"When's it on?" he asked.

"Saturday mornings at eight," Sasha said.

"Mmm," the doctor said. "That's when I'm on the tennis court."

"It's okay," Sasha said, as though he was apologizing.

"Tomorrow at noon?" he asked, confirming.

She couldn't. She'd missed too many hours already. She needed to be present at work, emotionally and physically. But how was she going to do that? Her life had suddenly tilted off its axis. She needed time, more time, to process. She wanted to get home to her list and a hot bath. Instead, she had to practice scatting in front of an unrehearsed band.

"It's not going to work tomorrow," she said. A heavy swell of disappointment emanated from Rusmeuth; she could feel it.

"Okay," he said. "Since you can't be here tomorrow, why don't you go into the room next door and change into a gown. I'd like to do a quick examination now."

Sasha had never been to a male gynecologist. Was he even a gynecologist? He said he specialized in men's fertility issues. What if he didn't know how to do a pelvic? She'd read about male doctors penetrating their patients and the patients not knowing what had happened.

"Can she come with us?" Sasha asked, pointing to the front-desk lady.

"I'm afraid MaryAnne's responsible for the phones," Rusmeuth said.

Sasha pictured the doctor penetrating her, holding her arms back and covering her mouth with a surgical glove. She didn't know why these images were so vivid, so palpable. She started crying again. She saw Rusmeuth and the lady exchange glances.

"Fine," he finally said. "We'll make this one exception."

~ ~ ~

As Sasha exited the building, she spotted a red Jeep whizzing by. The driver had a mop of curly hair—brown, messy. There was something about the hair. The car was going too fast for her to see a face. Melanie wouldn't have had the nerve to follow her here, would she? Melanie's journalistic endeavors wouldn't involve tailing her subject, would they? Sasha couldn't worry about it. Every time the thought surfaced, she pushed it far, far back. "Don't go there," she told herself sternly.

six

That night, when Sasha pulled into her driveway, she thought she saw Erika's black Volvo parked in front of her building. It reminded her that she hadn't called Erika since the night of the shower. It wasn't like her. But over the past few days things had been so crazy, so out of whack, that she just couldn't bear to get on the phone and pretend that it was business as usual.

Sasha gathered her bag, her overflowing date book, her cell phone, and her sweater and hoisted herself out of the car. Jordan and Erika were lingering in front of her apartment. The sweater fell out of her arms as soon as she saw them.

"She's here!" Erika said, clearly cutting off whatever Jordan was in the middle of telling her.

Earlier, Sasha had phoned Jordan from the car after her appointment with Rusmeuth. It was her third call to him in three days. She apologized for stalking him, as she put it, trying to add a little levity to the situation. She gave him the

Reader's Digest version of her visit with Dr. Rusmeuth. He was stunned, confused, suspicious. She explained that they both didn't need to feel these things, so why didn't he leave the worrying to her and he could just be there as the cheerleader? He agreed, quicker than she ever thought possible. He didn't even say anything about "the plan."

What she needed him for now would be a fun project. She told him about the list of sexual partners she had to create. She turned it into a game. Didn't it sound fun? He laughed, sort of, and promised he'd come over. Was she sure she didn't want to call her parents? Or Erika? Or anyone else? Yes, she was positive. Right now Jordan was the only one, outside her two doctors and their staff and perhaps the staff's family, but hopefully not, who knew, and she wanted to keep it that way.

So when she approached her front door and spotted Jordan and Erika, she was both grateful and angry. "Erika," she said, looking at Jordan.

"Don't be mad at him," Erika said. "He did the right thing by telling me. You can't go through this alone."

Sasha could feel Jordan watching her, but she focused her gaze on Erika and her pregnant belly.

"Sash, I want to be here for you. Even if you don't want me."

It wasn't that Sasha didn't want her—Erika was her oldest friend. It was more that she was still going through the process of digesting all the information. She wasn't sure how many people she wanted in on this. Erika would inevitably tell her husband, and probably her brother and her parents, and that would spawn a whole new batch of people who knew.

Sasha picked up her sweater and unlocked the front door. She knew Jordan and Erika were exchanging glances behind her. They followed her into the apartment. She wanted to break the awkwardness, but she wasn't quite sure what to say.

Inside, Sasha went about her business as though her friends weren't there. She flipped through her mail, checked messages, watered a few dying plants. "So, who's ready to trace my love life?" she finally asked, and both Erika and Jordan emitted nervous laughs.

Erika used this moment as a way in. "This has got to be such a trip for you! Quite frankly, it makes no sense, but—"

Out of the corner of her eye, Sasha saw Jordan nudge Erika. She was surprised to see the gesture, and also to see that it worked. Erika suddenly stopped talking. Seeing the two of them at her front door together had been almost as alarming as hearing that she was pregnant. They were from such different parts of her life: Erika from kindergarten, and only kindergarten, before Erika's family had moved from Boston to L.A. but they'd managed, miraculously, to keep in touch; and Jordan from day one of college, after the student-housing computer had thought "Sasha" was a boy's name and accidentally put them together as roommates. She would have been happy to live with Jordan, but the room was a quad and the others, Rich and Moses, had freaked her out. They'd had a good laugh and Jordan had begged her to stay, but rooming with three guys seemed more like a bad sitcom premise than real life. After a few phone calls, she had moved down the hall with Katie and Diane.

Erika and Jordan knew each other, but Sasha was positive that this must have been the first phone call they'd ever exchanged. She didn't know how she felt about it, but she did know that they were with her now. And when, if not now, would Sasha really need her friends?

~ ~ ~

Pen poised and ready to go, Erika started them off, sounding like a bingo announcer. "Loss of virginity: Randy McCall." They were sitting at the dining-room table. Sasha smiled and wrote the name down at the top of a blank piece of paper.

"Are we going in chronological order?" Jordan asked. "Or is this more of a free-for-all?"

"First we brainstorm, then we assemble an order," Erika said.

Jordan nodded. "John Robinson and that professor from graduate school."

"Javed Rimposhe," Erika said.

Sasha was impressed. "You remembered his first name?"

"How could I forget 'Javed'?"

Sasha added the names to her list.

"That guy," Jordan said, remembering someone.

"That's a little vague," Erika said. "We need first and preferably last names."

Sasha rolled her eyes. "I've known everyone's last name."

Erika had married her freshman-year boyfriend—the same boy to whom she had lost her virginity, and Sasha wondered if she was humbled or disgusted by the ever-growing list.

"That guy, you know . . . that guy with the hair and the glasses. The one who looked like Penn. Or was it Teller?" Jordan said.

Sasha knew immediately. "I never, ever, slept with Billy Lambert. I never even kissed him!"

"I've never even heard of him," Erika said, as though he was a rock star.

"He was one of Sasha's *intense* friendships," Jordan explained, a tinge of jealousy in his voice.

They all paused in thought for a moment. Then, "Matt Miller," Jordan and Erika said at the same time. Sasha wrote it down. He was her sophomore- and junior-year boyfriend, and he had broken up with her on the last day of summer vacation. She could still feel the sting. She had no idea where he was or what had become of him.

"Oren Schwartz," Sasha said, writing it down. Her list now numbered five. Erika looked at her quizzically. "Matt's best friend," Sasha explained. "Rebound."

"Yeah," Erika said, figuring it out.

"Oh, wait!" Sasha said, as though she were tapping into some psychic energy. "I did have intercourse with Billy Lambert's friend—Chad? That might be a last name I don't know."

"Have intercourse?" Jordan asked.

"Shut up," she said, flicking his shoulder. She wrote *Chad* with a blank line next to it. "And now we move on to grad school."

"But we're still brainstorming, we're not going in order," Erika reminded her.

"That's all there is," Sasha said.

"Boy, if I was Sean Avery I'd be pissed right about now," Jordan said.

Sasha covered her mouth. She'd skipped right over Sean. A two-year relationship lost in the abyss.

"That was telling," Erika said, never having liked him.

"How could I forget a person I had sex with every night for two years?" Sasha asked, not expecting an answer.

"You mean had *intercourse,*" Jordan corrected.

"Every night?" Erika asked.

Sasha nodded.

In an uncharacteristic move Erika said, "I have to tell you, I'm getting horny from all this sex talk."

"How can I help?" Jordan asked.

Sasha laughed, but she wasn't sure how she felt about them flirting. She didn't realize how much fun she was having until Erika announced that she had to go. She was having dinner at her mom's house.

"I know she's your mom," Sasha said, walking her to the front door, "but I'm begging you not to tell her."

"Promise," Erika said unconvincingly.

"More than promise?"

"I more than promise!" Erika said. Suddenly they were little girls again: *Super-duper more than promise.*

"We love you," Erika said, referring to herself and her fetus. It was something she had done ever since becoming pregnant.

"We love you, too," Sasha said, now looking down at her own belly. No, that sounded wrong. She sounded too attached. She wasn't a "we." She was an "I" plus a question mark. A giant, curly question mark with a huge splat of a period underneath. She modified her statement to Erika. "*I* love you, too."

Jordan almost followed Erika out the door, but Sasha pinched him hard enough so that he knew he had to stay. Closing the door, Sasha said, "There's someone else I need to add to the list." She sounded ashamed, remorseful. Before Jordan could guess, she told him. "Blake. Blake Gordon." Erika's brother.

seven

Fridays were tape days—two tapings, to be exact: a dress rehearsal with an audience in the afternoon, and the real thing in the early evening. Fridays were hectic, rushed, exhilarating, and just plain exhausting. Sasha made a beeline for her dressing room. She'd felt nauseous in the car ride over, and suddenly she had to get to the bathroom. She pushed her door open and ran past Melanie, who was supine on the couch. She made it to the toilet just in time. The sound of herself throwing up made her cringe. It was loud and violent, and she knew she could not emerge with her dignity intact.

When she finally went out, Melanie was sitting up on the couch, her eyebrows in a sad arch. "Are you going to be okay?" she asked.

Sasha lied by nodding. "Tape days always stress me out," she said. This was true, but not to the point of vomiting.

Melanie dug through her bag and extracted her legal steno pad. She jotted down a few things. Everything about Melanie was so tight and rigid and serious. There was no way she drove such a carefree, sexy Jeep. Sasha figured that now was as good a time as any to find out.

"What kind of car do you have?" she asked casually.

Melanie looked up from her writing. "A Jeep. Why?"

Sasha tried to contain her alarm. "Red?"

"Yeah. Red, topless. Why?"

"I was just admiring it outside in the parking lot."

Melanie looked confused. "I'm not in the lot. I'm on the street."

"Then I guess it's someone else's."

Melanie wouldn't stop. "Someone else has a red, topless Jeep here? Who? Who do you think?" She stood up, perhaps to go to investigate, but Sasha held her hand out.

"Don't worry about it," she said in a blow-off tone. "We've got some time. Why don't we use it wisely?"

Melanie adjusted herself back on the couch and Sasha dragged a chair over next to her. She forced a smile. "If you've got questions, I've got answers."

"Oh, I've got questions."

~ ~ ~

Sasha was ashamed to leave work again, but she'd finally made her second appointment with Dr. Rusmeuth for that afternoon, so she sneaked out after planting various alibis. She told Pam, the head writer, that she'd be resting in her dressing room. She told Steve, her director, that she'd be eating with Pam. She told Fritz, a coworker, that she was running out to grab something with Pam, and she told Melanie she'd be rehearsing with Fritz and to please not bother them. Then she ran to her car and headed to Dr. Rusmeuth's.

When she arrived, twenty minutes later, it was the doctor who was behind the reception window. They walked back to his office and Sasha presented her piece of paper, the eight names of her sexual partners. Dr. Rusmeuth looked it over.

"That's it?" he said, turning the paper over. "There are no more?"

Sasha suddenly felt inadequate. She didn't know how to answer. Rusmeuth shook his head. "I'm just relieved," he said. "How many do we have here?" He counted under his breath. ". . . six, seven, eight." He looked up at her. "Fantastic."

It felt absurd, being praised for remembering her sex life.

"Now comes the tricky part," Rusmeuth said. Was there anything trickier than this pregnancy? "We're going to need blood and perhaps tissue samples from these men."

Sasha fell back into the chair behind her. "Blood samples?" She didn't speak to half of these men anymore. She couldn't be bothered to track them down; that would be a full-time job, and she already had one of those. "Listen," she said, her voice shaking. "I'm afraid I don't have time for any of this."

Rusmeuth explained that he'd thought the numbers would be higher—fifteen, twenty, twenty-five, so having only eight came as a huge relief. "The only thing *not* on our side is time," he said.

Sasha thought back to six months ago when Erika had first told her she was pregnant. That week, Sasha had canceled dinner plans three times owing to late nights at work, and one day Erika had just appeared at the studio. Sasha was rehearsing some dance moves with a choreographer when she saw Erika standing out in the audience. Her first thought was that something horrible had happened—why else would Erika show up in the middle of the day? But upon closer inspection she noticed that Erika looked incredibly happy, effervescent even. It reassured her that this was probably just a friendly visit.

"I can't hold it in anymore," Erika said as they walked over to craft services to get some coffee. "I'm having a baby!"

Sasha heard the words, understood their meaning, and gasped for joy, but at that moment she took them literally and asked, "You and Jeff?"

Erika looked at her funny. "Are you kidding?" she'd asked.

Sasha smiled as she thought about it now. What a thing to say. At the time, it felt so strange hearing "I'm having a baby." I, singular.

Erika would make a great mom and Jeff a doting dad. It had always been a part of their plan. It fit the shape of their lives. The shape of Sasha's life was less formed, less clear. She didn't feel the same pressure to hit the same marks; she appreciated her freedom from conventionality. How could she explain this to a doctor? Did she even have to?

"As a doctor, my responsibility is to science," Rusmeuth was saying. "So when I encounter a case such as yours, I feel it's my responsibility and, quite frankly your responsibility, at least to explore it, probe it, question it. If not for you personally, then for larger, global reasons."

"Blood samples?" Sasha repeated, incredulous. That would mean getting in touch with them—her boyfriends, lovers, whatever—and trying to explain the utterly unbelievable circumstances in which she now found herself. She was moving forward in so many aspects of her life, why would she want to step backward? The task had about as much appeal as a root canal. Sure, she was curious about Matt Miller, John Robinson, Javed. According to Dr. Rusmeuth, someone, somewhere along the line, had deposited a lazy sperm. Who had it been?

Of course she was dying to know. "Most of them don't live here," she stammered. "I'm from Boston and I went to school in New York and . . ."

"They can draw blood in their home state and fax me the results."

"What are those blood results supposed to yield?" she asked.

"We'll be able to match their DNA with your fetus's DNA. The blood results will yield paternity."

"Is it one hundred percent guaranteed?" Sasha asked.

"It's ninety-nine point ninety-nine percent probability of paternity for inclusions, but one hundred percent certainty for exclusions."

P.O.E., Sasha thought to herself. Process of elimination. It was the method suggested for the GRE, the standardized test for graduate school. If you couldn't be certain of an answer, you used the process of elimination. It had worked. Sasha had scored very well.

"We can also do a buccal swab, where we swab saliva from the cheek, but I'd prefer blood," Rusmeuth said. "And I need to stress the importance of this happening ASAP."

Sasha imagined a phone call to Randy McCall, her first. She still kept in touch with him, but rarely. "Hi, Randy? It's Sasha Salter. I'm calling because I'm pregnant from a lazy sperm and there's a one-in-eight chance the baby's yours." Oh God, this wasn't happening. Only it was.

~ ~ ~

On her drive back to the studio, Sasha phoned Dr. Banks, who took the call immediately. "Do you perform abortions?" she asked, bypassing any pleasantries.

"I don't," Dr. Banks said.

"But you could refer me to someone, right?"

"Of course. My partner, Dr. Tucker, would be available for that procedure."

Wouldn't that make the most sense? Sasha thought to herself. It wasn't an easy answer, but it was an answer. It would certainly save her from eight daunting phone calls, more visits with Dr. Rusmeuth, more visits with Dr. Banks.

"Did something happen at Dr. Rusmeuth's today?" Dr. Banks asked.

"It's not just today," Sasha said. "It's yesterday, and the day before, and it's tomorrow and the day after. This is ruining my life."

"It's your body and your decision," Dr. Banks said calmly. "I just don't want it to be made as a panic response."

Sasha sighed. She understood. "Then I'll take some time to think about it," she said.

"You do that," Dr. Banks said. "And don't hesitate to call."

~ ~ ~

Sasha pulled into her space in the lot. She opened her front door and *pop!* Melanie appeared. "I thought you were with Fritz," she said. "And he thought you were with Pam."

Sasha gathered her belongings from the passenger seat and headed out of the lot. She wanted to swat Melanie. "What's up?" she asked instead.

Melanie walked at a faster pace to keep up. "It's just . . . y'know my time's important, too," she said. "And as you know it's quite an honor being picked for this feature—I mean, for you—and I just don't think you're giving me the respect I deserve as a journalist."

Sasha wondered if Melanie had practiced her little speech or if she was the kind of girl who easily expressed her concerns, no matter who the person or what the situation. She didn't seem nervous. Edgy, but not nervous.

"If you want to reschedule this for another week, let's talk about doing that," Melanie said after a few moments of silence. Sasha was still wearing her sunglasses, so she was able to widen her eyes in annoyance without Melanie seeing. They walked to the door of the soundstage. The guard winked and let them in. Inside, everything was pitch-black. Sasha loved feeling like she was in the dark. She stopped walking and took the time to speak.

"Listen, Melissa," she said, knowing that wasn't her name and trying purposely to flex some power muscle.

"Melanie!" Melanie said, astounded at the mistake.

"Melanie, we've had many deep, exhilarating conversations, at least in my memory. If I'm not here at lunch every now and then, and if I'm unable to rearrange my social schedule in the evenings sometimes, you'll have to understand. You don't need to be with me twenty-four hours a day literally," she said. "You're a writer. If you're not getting the whole picture, fill in the blanks."

At first, Melanie looked as though she'd been slapped in the face. In order to get a better look, Sasha took off her sunglasses. What she hadn't seen was that Melanie's face had contorted into a blushing, fuming red. Sasha felt the divide between them. It didn't have to be this way, and normally it wouldn't be. Normally Sasha wouldn't be worrying about blood and tissue samples from her sexual partners, either. She wanted to soften the situation, but she didn't have time. She had to call Jordan and give him the update.

"I need ten minutes alone," she told a pouting Melanie. "Ten minutes and then we can talk for . . ." She looked at her watch. "Half an hour. Then I need to be on the set." Melanie took off her own glasses and pressed her eyebrows together with her fingers. Sasha imagined this was a gesture she'd picked up from her boss, perhaps. An *Oh, life is so hard* moment.

"Okay," she finally said, replacing her glasses. "See you in ten."

Sasha knew Melanie would arrive in exactly ten minutes, so she picked up her pace and started dialing Jordan on her cell phone. She was surprised when his machine picked up. Lately he'd been home during the days, his business now a well-oiled machine. She unlocked her dressing room as she left a message. "Latest," she said. "I have to get blood samples from all my lovers. Yes, you heard right. Blood samples. From lovers. This oughtta be fun. What are you doing this weekend?"

Ever since Sasha had known him, Jordan's passion had been creating video games. He spoke the language—was it HTML? CIGI? JAVA? Whatever it was, Jordan knew it, knew how to design it, manipulate it, create text and characters with it. As soon as he moved to L.A., however, he tripped into a business that proved too hard to give up. His friend Dean sold promotional items and invited Jordan to help out until he found a job. Five years later, Jordan was co-owner of a thriving business. Hats, T-shirts, pens, and key chains for sports teams and the latest Hollywood blockbusters were flying off the shelves, and their client list was so extensive that they had to put a cap on it. Financially, Jordan was thriving, but creatively he felt stifled. Video-game companies were starting to pop up everywhere, yet he was mired in the mundane. He referred to himself as the middleman. "The middleman can always be eliminated," he'd say.

"But until you are, just laugh your way to the bank," Sasha said back.

Every time they found themselves getting money at an ATM, Jordan would double over in fake laughter.

"I get it, I get it," Sasha would say.

She had to admit that she was grateful for his flexible schedule, especially now, though normally she was the one constantly encouraging him to move in the direction of his passion. She'd even accompanied him to the E3 convention last year—an event so visually and audibly stimulating that she had to excuse herself and sit by the food court to regain her composure. In graduate school, they'd always talked about how detrimental video games were to kids, and now there she was in the epicenter. She remembered being able to tell that day how much he wanted to be a part of that world; his eyes lit up with excitement. His passion both thrilled and embarrassed her.

Once inside her dressing room, she flipped through the latest version of the script. Whenever the new drafts were delivered, they came in different-colored papers. The final draft was a rainbow of pinks, blues, and yellows. She licked her index finger and turned the pages, smiling at the jokes. At the top of each page was a header that read "Please Pass the Salter—Final." In terms of work, this Friday was no different from the last. A knock sounded on her door. No way had she been in there ten minutes. "What?" she called out, snappish. A muffled voice called back, "You have a visitor." She stood up, annoyed at being interrupted during her time alone. But it was Jordan. He stood outside her door looking a little dopey and embarrassed. He was holding a bouquet of daisies, her favorite. She took the flowers and he followed her to the couch.

"How did you know these are my favorite flowers?" she asked.

"How could I not know?"

"I'm so touched," she said. "Really."

"Well, you've had a hard couple of days."

"You wanna stay for the show?" she asked, assuming he would.

"Can't. Date."

"Ooh, same girl?"

"Echo."

"Like the echo, echo, echo. You like her?"

"She's . . ." He searched for the word. "Unusual. But in a good way."

"You like unusual."

"What's that supposed to mean?"

Sasha looked at the flowers. "Why don't you take these to her?" she asked.

"Because they're for you."

Jordan picked up the script and thumbed through it without stopping to read anything. Sasha suddenly felt insulted by his lack of interest. She looked at him. He had the kind of face that hadn't changed since he was a baby—round blue eyes, devilish smile, freckles dotting his nose and cheeks. He looked sly, as though he was constantly on the verge of playing a practical joke. She'd always thought that, from the day she met him.

"What?" he asked, catching her gaze.

"Nothing. It's just cool that you're here," she said.

And then came the knock. And then came Melanie. She seemed startled to see a man in the dressing room—a man she didn't recognize. She approached him with her hand outstretched.

"Melanie," she said, shaking his.

Sasha hadn't even told Jordan about the article. She tried to fill him in. "Melanie's a journalist writing an article called '20 Under 30—Ones to Watch.' She's hanging out for a week."

"I'm *shadowing* Sasha for a week," Melanie corrected.

Jordan immediately understood the severity of the situation. "Ooh," he said.

"We've got half an hour," Sasha reminded Melanie. "You can stay if you want," she told Jordan.

"That's okay. She doesn't want to shadow me."

He stood up and dropped the script back on the table. He extended his arms for a hug, and Sasha complied. Melanie stood close, watching.

"Have fun tonight. See you tomorrow?"

"See you tomorrow."

Jordan walked out of the dressing room, leaving Sasha with a fleeting sadness. She took a bottle of water from the minifridge.

"Want one?" she asked Melanie.

She shook her head. "Is that your boyfriend?" she asked.

Sasha laughed. "No, that's Jordan."

"And Jordan is your . . ."

"Friend."

"Mmm-hmm," Melanie said, reaching into her bag for her folders.

Sasha joined her on the couch. She uncapped the bottle and started gulping down the water. She hadn't realized how thirsty she was until she tasted the first sip.

"Are daisies your favorite flowers?" Melanie asked, gazing at them.

"Yes," Sasha answered. She set the bottle down and stuck a few flowers into the remaining water.

"What's your favorite color?" Melanie asked.

"Green."

"Dog or cat person?"

"Cat."

"Silver or gold?"

"What's my favorite precious metal?" Sasha said. "Silver."

"Do you want children one day?" Melanie sniffed as she asked.

"One day," Sasha said, staring directly into Melanie's boring brown eyes. "Do you?"

"I haven't decided," Melanie said, turning the page. "Coffee or tea?"

"Tea."

Their games continued until the director called Sasha to the set.

eight

It was the weekend, blissfully the weekend. Sasha put her all into the final eight hours of work. She dazzled at dress rehearsal, killed at the final taping. Perfecting her Big Red waddle, she snapped her fingers as she jazz-scatted the alphabet. She offered herself up to Melanie at any and all free moments. When she took her bows at the end of the show, she made sure her hair dangled over her face as she came up, sending the kids into joyful giggles. She charmed the kids and their parents; she posed, employing her new practiced smile, for photo after photo. She shook hands, like Oprah, as the audience filed out. She made sure Melanie was with her and laughed with delight as the kids shook Melanie's hand, too. Lewis Adler, the network executive, even tapped her on the shoulder and extended his arms for a hug. "Amazing, kiddo," he said. She'd never seen him that friendly. The weekend, too, welcomed her with open arms, and she was more than ready to fall in.

All week the idea of an abortion had nagged at the back of her mind like a pushy aunt. "Just do it, just do it—what are you waiting for?" it persisted. "People have done it—it's not the end of the world. Move on with your life." But weighing on her mind was the idea that perhaps there was a grander reason for all of this. Sasha wondered what would happen if she were to shift her attitude, jump aboard the surreal train, and see where it took her. In the fleeting moments when she was able to open herself up to the possibility, she found that a part of her was curious. What if she and one of these men had actually spawned a child? She decided against calling Dr. Banks back, at least for now. She decided, instead, to track down the men, which seemed the only way to either prove or disprove Dr. Rusmeuth's absurd hypothesis.

Sasha held a green felt-tip pen in her hand as she circled the names of the boys—or were they men now?—she was going to call first. Randy McCall, Blake, and Sean. These were people she was still in touch with, people she had easy access to. The others would prove more difficult. Javed was still a professor at the university, but they hadn't spoken since her graduation. John Robinson, Matt, Oren, Chad—they were more elusive. She looked at the names and then finally circled John and Matt. They could be found, probably through old phone books or mutual friends.

Jordan was coming over at noon and Erika at two. It was only seven in the morning, and Sasha now had five hours to busy herself. Maybe she should break the ice and make a call. That way, when her friends arrived she would already have some sense of accomplishment. The more she thought about it, alone and curled in her blankets, the more it seemed a great idea. Since it was seven in Los Angeles, it was ten in Boston, and what better time than ten on a Saturday morning to hear that someone you slept with eleven years ago might be carrying your child.

Sasha emerged from her sheets, hair matted, nightgown twisted around her legs. She walked into the living room and picked up the Palm Pilot she rarely used. She found Randy's name in a matter of seconds. Before calling, she propped up the pillows behind her so that she was sitting upright. She didn't want to sound sleepy. She cleared her throat and rehearsed out loud. "Randy? Hey!!!" (Too enthusiastic.) "Randy, it's Sasha." (Too serious.) "Hey, Randy. Surprise! It's Sasha Salter." That worked. The word *surprise* would be an appropriate foreshadowing of the other surprise to follow. She took a deep breath and dialed the number.

Randy had never been a good friend, but he had been a constant in Sasha's life for as long as she could remember. He'd grown up around the block from her, and their parents had been friendly. He came from a family of five brothers—some older, some younger—and because of this Sasha had always been intrigued by his household. She was an only child, and the bustle of his home was in stark contrast to the quiet of hers.

The boys had all attended Bishop's Catholic School, but in eleventh grade Randy transferred to Sasha's public school. By then she was so tired of her group of friends that she welcomed Randy as a strange and needed relief. Randy was already driving, and one day at lunch he offered to drive Sasha to school the next day. She usually walked with some girlfriends, but she was ready for a change and accepted his offer. She enjoyed the rides to school, less than two miles away, especially in winter. His car smelled exactly like his house, and Sasha breathed in the curious scent. They never ran out of things to talk about, but in Sasha's opinion they never established an intimate friendship, either.

In March, inspired by her friends' sexual activities, Sasha thought she should have some of her own. Randy wasn't even her idea. She had a nagging crush on Brad Leavitt, who was a year younger and on the track team. She fantasized about his lean body sliding up against hers, and then later in the fantasy she was trackside, cheering him on. But she didn't know Brad—had no relationship whatsoever with him. It was Miranda who suggested Randy, or, rather, "That guy you always drive with." Once the idea was planted it grew, and Sasha was well aware that her attitude had shifted from fun-time neighbor to schoolgirl crush. She started wearing eyeliner and longer, more dangly earrings. She marveled at the way it seemed to work. He started touching her more, punctuating stories with a slap on the arm or a touch of the leg. They even started sitting in his car once they'd reached their destination, finding endless things to talk about. They started calling each other, relating mundane stories that momentarily seemed interesting.

It finally took place in his parents' bed. It was after a track meet they'd both attended, Randy to photograph the event and Sasha to scope out Brad Leavitt. He offered to drive her home, then suggested that she come to his house. They watched *Grease* in the basement, then kissed, drank beer, and went upstairs into his parents' room, which smelled exactly like his car, and in the dark, quietly, she lost her virginity.

Sasha had always been paranoid about pregnancy, especially during her first time. As a kid, she'd watched one too many movies-of-the-week; the ones that depicted poised, prim girls who had made the mistake of having sex at a young age and were now saddled with decisions about abortions or child rearing, while their friends were deciding between dresses for the prom.

That first time in his parents' bed, when Sasha could feel Randy against her, solid and firm, she asked if he wouldn't mind wearing two condoms.

"Two?" he asked. "Are you serious?"

She was serious. It wasn't that much of an imposition, was it? They were thin little things, those condoms. If one broke, there would be another to catch the overflow.

"I can always pull out," Randy suggested, a slight pleading in his voice.

"No, thanks," Sasha said, as though he'd just offered her a piece of gum. She wanted to go to her prom thin and childless.

Randy had obliged with the two-condom request, and then later, when one of Sasha's friends told her about spermicide, it was added to their routine. No Babies Having Babies for me, thank you very much, she had thought, referring to one of the more memorable specials.

Years later, Randy held an arbitrary place in Sasha's life. They were still connected, but merely by a thread.

"This is Randy," he said, answering the phone. He still lived in Boston, and whereas Sasha had lost all traces of her accent, Randy's had somehow become magnified.

"This is Sasha," she said. Not in the rehearsal.

"Sasha!" he said. "Are you in town?"

"No, I'm not," she said. Suddenly she had the shakes. Her mouth went dry and her voice dropped an octave. "How are you?" she asked robotically.

"I'm doing good! I was just going to play ball with the guys," he said. She assumed the guys were his brothers. Then he added, "I missed your show this morning. I slept in."

"That's okay. That's not why I'm calling."

"But I saw it last week. Adorable. My nephews love it."

Randy's brothers all had sons. Randy was single, last she'd heard, but was dating a flight attendant.

"So, this is kind of cuckoo," Sasha started. She was glad she was in bed because she was feeling light-headed. Another wave of *this can't be happening* washed over her.

"Yeah?"

"I've got this medical situation," she said. "This medical *anomaly*."

"Are you sick, Sasha?"

"No, no, not that. It seems that, for some strange reason, not the normal reason, but another rare, bizarre—"

"Sasha. What's wrong?" he interrupted.

"Oh, it's not terrible, really. See, apparently I'm pregnant and—"

"Holy shit! Congratulations! Who's the lucky guy?"

"Well, that's the problem."

He was suddenly silent.

"Since I haven't been active, sexually, in a couple of, um, years, there's some confusion as to what's going on."

More silence.

"This is totally freaky," she said, assuming that's what he was thinking. And then, "Hello?"

"I'm here," he said. "I'm just—whoa."

"I know. Whoa. I'm working with a doctor who thinks the pregnancy could have been, um, delayed . . . from a while back, and he suggested I get blood or tissue samples from anyone I've ever been involved with," she said. "You're my first call."

She heard a dog bark in the background.

"Bruiser!" Randy called. "Hold up!"

"Are you still dating that flight attendant?" Sasha asked.

"I'm talking to the dog."

"I know. I'm asking independently of this conversation."

"Are you telling me it could be mine? Sasha, it's not possible."

Sasha looked out her bedroom window toward the California sunshine. Back in Boston she pictured snow piled high. She imagined the cold, the freeze-your-sinuses cold; the deep chill of February.

"Would you be willing to take a blood test?" she asked. "If I could just get the ball rolling on this, y'know?"

The dog barked again. And then she heard a sigh.

"You can't tell your parents, though," she added. "I haven't even told mine yet."

"Are you kidding? I'm not telling anybody. Sasha, there's got to be something you're leaving out."

"Nothing," Sasha said. "You know everything I know. Oh, except it happens with bats."

"What?"

"Delayed fertilization. Bats store sperm through the winter. I never knew that, did you?"

"Through the winter?" Randy said. "But if it was me it would be through *ten* winters."

They were quiet again until Randy said, "Okay. So how do I give you blood?"

"You go to your local hospital. Mass General?"

"Beth Israel," Randy corrected.

"And you tell them you need a DNA blood test. My doctor's requesting it. His name is Dr. Rusmeuth. Ira Rusmeuth."

"Hold on, I've got to get a pen."

Sasha paused until he returned.

"Okay, go on," he said.

"Give them the code DNA 827. That way, it goes on Dr. Rusmeuth's bill as a research expense."

"I hate needles," Randy said.

"I'm sorry," Sasha said. She meant it. There was nothing worse than getting pricked when you didn't need to be. "It's just like giving blood at the doctor's. It's not gonna be long and drawn out." At least she didn't think it would be.

It was awkward hanging up. She wasn't quite sure how to end the conversation. "Are you okay?" she asked him.

"I'm wondering if *you're* okay," he said.

When they finally did hang up, Sasha started crying again. She took a red felt-tip pen and crossed his name off the list. High on the adrenaline of completing the first call, she wanted to make another one, but it was close to eight and her show was about to start.

When it debuted a year and a half ago, she'd arranged a slumber party so they could wake up the next morning and watch. She'd invited Erika and her husband, Jeff, and her brother, Blake, who'd just returned from a trial run of living in New York. She'd also invited Jordan and some friends from the show, Fritz, Ross, and Sarah. Her mom sent custom-made cookies in the shape of saltshakers. Erika acted as bartender and kept the drinks flowing—rum drinks for Sasha and Fritz, vodka for Blake and Jeff, wine for the others. Everyone woke up at seven forty-five the next morning, groggy and hungover, to watch the show. Sasha sat on the floor and leaned against Blake, who was on the couch. She felt a combination of ecstasy and modesty as it debuted. Erika kept squeezing her, Jordan flashed proud smiles, her coworkers hooted and hollered. When it ended, phone calls streamed in from various friends and relatives, and later that day, when her slumber party had departed, a flurry of e-mails arrived, some from her graduate-school friends, some from college friends. She'd felt connected and disconnected all at the same time.

~ ~ ~

From the time the show ended until eleven, Sasha fielded another slew of unexpected phone calls. The most surprising was Dr. Banks, who identified herself as Klara Banks, to which Sasha responded, "I'm sorry, you have the wrong number," and hung up. Only when the phone rang again did she realize that it was Dr. Banks, *the* Dr. Banks. She was checking in on Sasha. She'd been thinking about her and had been in touch with Dr. Rusmeuth. She also wanted to pass on the number of another doctor, a therapist, and she strongly recommended that Sasha get in touch with her. Sasha announced that she had already made one call, so the ball was rolling on that front. Dr. Banks ended their conversation by giving Sasha her home and pager numbers, which she scribbled on the back of a coffee receipt. "Is there anything else you'd like to ask me?" Dr. Banks asked.

Sasha thought about it. "I'm still not convinced that this can really happen," she said. And then, "I know that's not a question."

"The body *is* mysterious," Dr. Banks said. "We've only scratched the surface in terms of our understanding."

"But have you ever seen anything like this?" Sasha asked.

"Like this specifically? No. But I've seen many other conditions. Things that would make your hair stand on end."

Sasha didn't want to know. "Okay, here's another question," she said. "Should I tell my parents?"

"I don't know, Sasha," Dr. Banks started. "You could probably use all the support you can get right now. If your family can give that sort of support, despite these unusual circumstances, I'd say tell them. You shouldn't have to go through this alone. You can give them my number and I'd be happy to talk to them if they'd like."

"I'll think about it," Sasha said. "Thanks for calling. Sorry I hung up on you."

The next call was Jordan, saying in a whisper that he was running a little late and he'd be there closer to one, and then it was the *Los Angeles Times* trying to sell her the newspaper (she got it for free at work). Pam called after that, saying this was one of their best shows. She'd watched it with her niece, who was laughing hysterically. Sasha ignored the call-waiting tone and kept talking to Pam. When they finally hung up, she checked her messages and was relieved to hear that she had missed a call from Melanie. "I just want to say how awesome it was seeing the show after spending the better part of the week with you," she said. "So cool. Can't wait for next week. Oh, by the way, sorry for being—I don't know, grumpy or something yesterday. 'Kay? See ya. Oh, if your schedule opens up this weekend, give me a jingle."

High off the success of her show, and still feeling galvanized by the first phone call with Randy, Sasha found and thumbed through an old address book. It was a long shot, but she still had John Robinson's parents' phone number. They lived in Chicago. She boldly dialed the number. Mrs. Robinson, she assumed, answered. She had met her a few times when she had visited the college, but Sasha would definitely have to refresh her memory. She hoped they wouldn't get tangled in a long conversation. She only wanted John's number and then to move on to the next call.

John had been the dorm clown—always a smile and a warm

hug for everyone. She couldn't remember what he'd studied, but he'd always had a devilish glint in his eyes and Sasha had been attracted to his ringlets of black hair. In bed she would pull them down and watch as they magically sprang back. She had always yearned for curly hair and, quite frankly, found it wasted on a man. She remembered burrowing in his hair, breathing in the musky odor of patchouli.

"Hello, Mrs. Robinson," Sasha started. "I'm not sure if you remember me, but this is Sasha Salter." There was no response. "John's friend." Still no response. "From college." How many Sashas could he know? After what seemed like an excruciating silence, his mother finally spoke. She was clear and direct as she said, "Honey, John passed on last year."

nine

It was three in the afternoon. Sasha and Jordan were sitting on the couch, stunned by the news of John's death. Erika had spent the past half hour trying to comfort them.

"It's not even that I'm sad," Jordan said. "I'm just shocked."

"How could we not have heard?" Sasha asked for the third time.

John had been integral to their early college years but then later had faded into obscurity, or the drama clique or the druggies—she couldn't quite remember. A year after they met, John moved out of the dorms and into a shared apartment in the West Village. Every time she ran into him on campus, he was with another girl, and Sasha soon came to realize that their intentions were not mutual. She thought she had tripped into a relationship, and he was just passing through.

"Well, I hope the baby's not his," Erika said.

She'd only said what Sasha was thinking, but it annoyed her to hear it out loud. She glare-glanced at Erika.

"What?"

"You know what," Sasha said.

"I have to say something else," Erika said. "I know it might not be appropriate—"

"It can't be worse than your last comment," Sasha grumbled.

"I just think you're going about this all wrong. If I were you, I'd start with the most recent partner and work backward. What are the chances that this all really happened from a ten-year-old sperm?"

"According to Dr. Rusmeuth, it's possible."

"I think Erika's right," Jordan piped up. "I think Sean should be your next call."

Sasha whined, "I don't want to."

"Then I'll do it," Erika offered. She seemed sincerely eager. "Let's face it. If anyone's sperm is lazy, it's his."

Sasha wasn't dating him anymore and therefore, mercifully, didn't feel the need to defend him. She could see how he might be perceived as lazy, living at home as a twenty-four-year-old—a real *mamoni*, only he wasn't Italian. He had a full-time job looking for a job, and at that time in her life he had been good for her. The mechanics of her show were already in place and her ambition complemented his lack of it.

They had met at a party. Sean was in the living room rolling a joint and she was in the dining room, peering into the living room, wondering who the cute guy rolling the joint was. She was stressed and wanted a hit of it, so she'd approached him and they'd shared a skinny, wet joint while spilling forth their life stories, as often happened at parties with strangers in Los Angeles. He'd just moved back home after living in Iceland,

Alaska, and Nova Scotia for various ecological projects. At the time, stoned and lonely, she'd found him worldly. She had lived only in Boston, New York, Tucson, and now Los Angeles. He was living at home until he found a job, but it was cool, he explained, because his parents traveled a lot. Only after Sasha broke up with him, two years later, on the phone because he was too tired to come over, did he get a job, as a fraternity recruiter for his alma mater. He called her when he accepted the job, but at that point what did she care? She was knee-deep in her work, and it felt like too little too late to give him any credit.

If their relationship was built on anything, it was sexual activity. She would wake him up in the middle of the night just to satisfy him, and he would return the favor for hours and hours until they fell back asleep, only to wake up to more sex the next morning. Through their relationship, Sasha had reached the peak of her sexual confidence—no more doing it with the lights out, no more throwing on the bathrobe as soon as sunlight filtered in. She felt that he, too, had reached that same stage in his life, and that was why together they were endlessly energetic and uninhibited. In terms of quantity, it was certainly possible that little lazy mama's boy Sean had filled her body with the most sperm. She hated to give him the accolades, but it seemed logical.

"Call him," Jordan said.

"Yeah, just call," Erika agreed.

But now Sasha felt uncomfortable. They hated him. She didn't want them listening to her conversation.

"We'll go in the other room," Erika suggested. "Come on, Jordan."

Jordan got up off the couch and followed Erika into Sasha's bedroom. Sasha got the cordless phone and stayed in the kitchen to make the call. She knew his number by heart, because it ended in 2223. It was three fifteen on a Saturday afternoon. If he wasn't off luring some unsuspecting high-school student to Sigma Alpha whatever, he'd probably be home napping or smoking a joint. He answered, "Hi!" and Sasha's heart began to pound.

"Sean, it's Sasha."

"Oh. I was expecting someone else."

Sasha knew him well enough to know that he wanted her to ask who. "How are you?" she said instead.

"Things are *great*. I mean, *fabulous*. Really."

She knew for a fact that he would not ask about her. That had been the pattern of their relationship—her shoulder for him to lean on and not much but sex in return. After a lengthy pause on both ends, Sean finally said, "What can I do you for, Sasha?"

"Well, it's a really long story," she said, suddenly feeling weary from the day's events.

"I have time."

Of course he had time.

"I'm suddenly thinking we should meet," she said.

"Really? You can just tell me over the phone, you know."

"I know," she said, now certain that she wanted to see him in person—see his reaction, see a reminder of a recent relationship. "But I just think it's better if I tell you in person." She meant it. Maybe she'd even go with him to the hospital to draw the blood. She pictured walking into Dr. Rusmeuth's office on Monday, carrying a vial of Sean's electric-red blood, handing it over like an offering.

They made plans to meet the next day at a little place she knew near Cedars-Sinai; that way, she could deliver the news and then escort him over to Outpatient Services. They hung up and Sasha was about to run into her room to tell her friends when suddenly Erika emerged, holding a white piece of paper as if she were dangling a rat by its tail. Upon closer inspection, Sasha could see the green circles and thick red underlines of her "intercourse chart." Erika was expressionless.

"I don't remember the name *Blake* on your list," she said.

Behind her, Jordan's face was contorted into an expression that said things weren't going as planned.

ten

Erika stormed out, claiming that she felt duped. It was a dramatic reaction, especially for a woman who was eight months pregnant. Sasha tried to chase her, but she was moving at an alarming clip and Jordan called out for Sasha to let her go. She stood there in the middle of the walkway, watching Erika slam the car door. Suddenly she was starring in a real-life version of *As the World Turns*.

~ ~ ~

After Erika moved to Los Angeles, she and Sasha had maintained their friendship despite the distance. As kids they wrote pages and pages of letters, culminating in the Fifty-Page Letter in seventh grade. It was Erika's idea, embarking on a meaty letter detailing their daily lives. Sasha labored over hers, scribbling away at it every day as if it were a diary. It took her two months to finish the thing, explaining life at her new school, her friends, crushes, classes, and in return she received

Erika's letter. It came three months later and sadly, painfully, chronicled her parents' divorce. Sasha still had that letter, the paper now browned and crackly. Eventually their letters gave way to audiotapes, which alternated between music and talking. Sasha formatted hers like a radio show, introducing songs, playing them, and then casually chatting like a seasoned DJ.

For a high-school graduation present, their parents had chipped in for a trip to Paris and the girls, each blessed with four years of French, spent a week together visiting museums, dining out, hanging out with other travelers at the hostel, walking along the Seine, and anticipating the next chapter of their life: college. Sasha was heading to NYU and Erika to Berkeley. When they were kids they'd always fantasized about going to the same college, Princeton, not because it was an Ivy League school but because Brooke Shields had gone there and they both thought she was pretty.

Erika met Jeff her freshman year in college. Sasha had lost her virginity first, but Erika had fallen in love first, and they spent hours on the phone discussing it. They remained in touch throughout college, but not the way they had been in high school. During her junior year, Erika went back to Paris for a year abroad, but Sasha stayed in New York. She was having too much fun, plus she had done some falling in love of her own, with Matt.

Slowly, Sasha and Erika inched apart, not separating but forming their own identities. They became distinct where once they had been one. At Erika's wedding five years ago, Sasha had stood in the church in her bridesmaid uniform with four other girls and felt the distance. A few of the bridesmaids were from Berkeley, and one was a friend from Erika's graduate program in psychology. They all seemed to know one another, to connect. They spoke of their own weddings, honeymoons, when they wanted babies. Sasha was in graduate school, so removed from all these life events. She was knee-deep in an affair with her newly separated professor, for God's sake. She was absorbed in education and child psychology and learning. Everything else—weddings and babies in particular—seemed so tired and conventional. Still, she plastered on a smile, linked arms with Blake, and walked down the aisle.

When Sasha and Erika rejoined each other in Los Angeles a few years later, their relationship was infused with a new energy. They had such a vast shared history to draw on, but they were each also going forward in ways both interesting and unique—Erika as a marriage and family counselor and happily married to Jeff, Sasha as a single woman and the star of her creative thesis.

Sure they'd bickered on occasion, but they'd never really fought. On their trip to France Sasha had experimented with smoking, choking her way through packs of slim cigarettes, but feeling exceptionally cool in the process. Erika had constantly swatted smoke out of her face and clucked every time Sasha lit up.

"Who picks up smoking at eighteen?" Erika asked.

"I'm just trying it on for size," Sasha said.

"You going to try lung cancer on for size, too?"

This Blake incident would certainly go down as one of their most dramatic.

~ ~ ~

"She's just mad that neither of you told her," Jordan said. "You can't blame her, can you?"

"Jordan, I only slept with him four or five times," Sasha said.

"What if I slept with Erika? It would be the same thing.

She's like your sister, I'm like your brother. What if we slept together and didn't tell you and then you found out?"

"Did you?"

"See? You'd feel duped."

They went inside Sasha's apartment and sat down on the couch.

"Is it possible that *every* aspect of my life is in disarray?" Sasha wondered.

"Could be."

"Don't you think this is all too much for one person to handle?"

"Well, depends on how you look at it."

Sasha stretched her neck. "Oh, now you're telling me I have a bad attitude?"

"I just think this is the most freaky, fucked-up thing that could ever happen—and it's happening to you. How cool is that?"

Sasha laughed at his upbeat, positive attitude. She laughed and laughed, and Jordan looked at her and smiled.

~ ~ ~

Coffee with Sean didn't go as well as she'd expected. Anticipating that he would show up late, Sasha herself had shown up late only to find an impatient Sean, who, having gotten the time mixed up, had arrived twenty minutes early. He'd already downed a cup of coffee and was thumbing through the coupons of the Sunday paper.

"Hey," Sasha said. He didn't stand up to greet her; he just looked at her. "I can't see you behind those sunglasses." She sat down across from him. He immediately slid them up to the crown of his head and widened his eyes. "Okay, I see you," she said. "And I see you're mad."

He looked at his giant diver's watch and then at Sasha. "I guess I am mad," he said. "I've been here for forty minutes."

His grumpiness sent her mood spiraling downward. She could feel it.

"So, what's up? What's the big news?" he asked.

"I'm pregnant," she said without meaning to. It was all too quick. She hadn't eased into it as previously rehearsed.

Sean's eyes bugged, but the rest of his body language remained calm. "Congratulations," he offered.

They stared at each other for a little. Sasha hadn't seen him in more than a year, and in that time he had grayed around the temples. His sunglasses were sitting in a way that accentuated his ears. He looked alarmingly like Alfred E. Neuman. She shook away the thought and averted her eyes.

"Well, I know you're not telling me because it's mine," he said.

"That's the thing," Sasha started. It was all moving too fast. She felt it was heading in the direction of disaster. Suddenly a little girl, probably five years old, and her father approached the table.

"It's okay," the father was saying, nudging the girl toward Sasha. And then, "We're sorry to interrupt, but Brittany here wants to tell you something."

Sasha leaned away from Sean and toward the girl and her father. She could see Sean out of the corner of her eye. He was tilting backward in his chair and his sunglasses had slipped back down onto his face.

"Hi, Brittany," Sasha said, forcing a Cheshire-cat smile.

"Please pass the Salter," the little girl said, and then leaned into her father's leg and hid her face.

"Do you like the show?" Sasha asked. The girl stayed hidden.

"Does she like it? She loves it. Right, Britty? Honey, let go of my leg and talk to the nice lady."

"It's fun-ny," she said from behind her dad's leg.

"Thank you!" Sasha said.

"Cyva tograf?" the girl mumbled.

Her dad jerked his leg around until Brittany let go. "She wants your autograph," he clarified. "Britty, use your words."

Sasha dug through her purse, but she had neither paper nor pen. She looked up at Sean, who had gone back to reading the paper. "Do you have a pen?" she asked him.

He shook his head without looking up. A woman at the next table ran over with a notebook and a pen. "We love your show, too," she said. She was in her forties.

Sasha scribbled her name on the paper and then above it added, "To Brittany—thanks for watching!" She ripped the paper out of the spiral notebook, returned the notebook to its owner, and handed the paper to the girl's dad.

"Oh, Britty, look at that! What do you say to the nice lady?"

Brittany suddenly jumped up and declared, "Thank you."

"You're welcome!"

Brittany, infused with a new energy, jumped and jumped again. "Fun-ny, fun-ny, fun-ny," she said, and then doubled over in that contrived laughter only children can get away with.

Sasha smiled.

"Someone's chocolate biscotti is kicking in," the dad said. "Right, Britta Belly?"

Sasha was eager for them to leave, but they were still standing close. She was trying to contrive a way to express that their interaction was over without offending either of them when Sean slapped down the newspaper and cleared his throat.

"If you'll excuse us," he said, more to Brittany than to her father. The father shot Sean a pissed-off look and walked away with his daughter.

"That was rude," Sasha said. "They would have left."

"Oh, are you scolding me?" he asked. All of a sudden the two years had vanished, and there they were at the end of their relationship again.

"I'm not scolding you, I'm just tel—"

"You're pregnant," he said, louder than she'd have liked.

"Shh."

"It's a secret?"

They sparred like this until Sasha leaned in close and gave a condensed version of the situation. Sean's face twisted and contorted. At first he looked as if he were having an orgasm. Then he looked disgusted.

"Can we just run across the street and get some blood?" she asked, as though this were a normal suggestion.

"I'm meeting a date here," he said gruffly.

"Sean. Please?"

"Sasha, I said I'm meeting a date here." He looked at his watch. "In ten minutes."

Sasha sat back in her chair and crossed her arms. She felt tears welling up. They were so close to the hospital, so close to moving forward on this.

"I'd like to talk to my doctor about this before I agree to anything."

"Your doctor's not gonna know. He's not going to get it. This is extremely unusual."

"It doesn't add up," he said in a cautious tone.

Sasha tried her luck one more time. "So you won't just run across the street with me for five minutes? We'll tell the people who work here to look out for your date and tell her you'll be right back."

Sean pounded his hand on the table. "Fine," he said, much to her surprise.

"Fine, now?" she asked tentatively.

They stood up together and headed out the door.

~ ~ ~

The lines were longer than Sasha had anticipated, and for a while they sat there, Sean tapping his foot and Sasha feeling anxious about Sean's state. He excused himself to make a call on his cell, and when he returned he said his date was going shopping at the Beverly Center and when he was done he'd meet her there. Sasha suggested they keep this situation between them, and Sean looked at her. "Why would I ever tell someone about this?"

When Sean was finally called in, Sasha offered to go with him, but he refused. "DNA 827," she reminded him as he walked away.

"I know," he said, irritated.

Sasha wandered over to the hospital gift shop and browsed through the cards. She was looking for a sympathy card for John's mother. There were belated birthday and anniversary cards, but no belated sympathy cards. What if you found out about somebody's death a year later, as Sasha had? She settled on a simple card with flowers on the front; she'd fill it with some appropriate words.

Sasha's relationship with death included the loss of two grandparents—one before she was born and one when she was a toddler, and a classroom bunny she had come to love. Nevertheless, she had been aware of her own mortality from a young age, often dizzying herself trying to imagine what it would be like *not* to think.

She was stunned to learn that someone she knew had died. In death, where had he gone? She had been so drawn to John's liveliness. Everything about him had been larger than life. He laughed a little too loud, drank a little too much, fucked a little too hard. She realized now that he had probably been making his imprint. She wondered if, during those college years, he had sensed his fate. She presumed that it had been a suicide since his mom had mentioned something about him "succeeding this time."

How shocking it must have been for his mother to receive Sasha's call yesterday, casually asking for her dead son. Sasha's memory took her back to the Avalon in New York, where she and John had gone on a date to hear David Byrne. John stood behind her, his arms wrapped around her waist, their hips rocking to the music. She'd always felt warm and safe in his embrace, but also aware that if they rocked too much, so to speak, they might fall over.

He'd always taunted death in a way—wandering around the city at three in the morning, taking mind-numbing drugs—but death had caught him and dragged him to the underworld. She couldn't imagine that John was now still when so many of her memories were of him in motion.

He'd inspired her to take risks, too. She'd read once in a trashy magazine that men were turned on when women didn't wear underwear, so at an off-campus party she'd leaned over and said she wasn't wearing any. It took all her courage not to wear any in the first place and even more to whisper to him, *"I forgot my panties."* How could someone forget to put on her underwear, and how did she utter that horrible word *panties*? The look that registered in his eyes was so frightfully lustful that she regretted it as soon as she said it. Not long after that party he casually dropped out of her life, moved on, stopped hanging out, stopped calling. Now he was gone forever.

And here she was on the ground floor of a hospital, hidden from the goings-on upstairs—perhaps a heart surgery on the fourth floor, an anxious family huddled in the waiting room, or a cancer patient being fed the drippings of an IV. There were victims of a car accident—one moment alive in a joyride, the next dead in the emergency room. Death hovered over her, but so did life. A grandfather held his first granddaughter on the ninth floor. That's where Erika would be in a few weeks. Inside Sasha a life was forming, too, and there were no answers yet as to how, only questions as to whom.

~ ~ ~

When Sean exited, with a Band-Aid across his inner arm, she stood up. He looked dazed, a little like the walking wounded. "I gave him the fax number you gave me."

"Thanks."

He put his sunglasses back on. "I hate hospitals," he said.

Who didn't? She'd always hated the way he declared the obvious.

"Well, I'm off to the Beverly Center to meet Miriam."

Miriam?

"I appreciate this," she said, and leaned in to hug him. Her hands were around his shoulders and his were around her waist. It felt nice to be in someone's arms. She pressed into him and whispered, "You're alive." She could hear the muted beat of his heart. He immediately let her go and looked at her, cautious and confused. He waved as he left, and Sasha had the distinct feeling that this was the last time she'd ever see him: unless, of course, the sperm was his.

eleven

That Sunday night Sasha stumbled upon a welcome surprise. While flipping through some old journals from college, she realized that she'd never had sex with Oren Schwartz, Matt's best friend. They'd kissed and done some other stuff, but no *penetration*. She'd built up a sexual relationship with him in her head, mainly to get back at Matt for dumping her. She took a black pen and crossed his name off the list. Two down, one dead, five to go.

Sasha looked at the clock radio and thought about calling Erika. They hadn't spoken since she stormed out of the house the day before. She understood why Erika felt betrayed, but it had been so many years ago.

Blake was four years younger than Erika. Sasha remembered him as an infant and then later as a toddler who followed Erika everywhere. Blake the toddler had grown up into Blake the Boy Scout, Blake the baseball player, Blake the drummer, the philosophy major, the motorcycle rider.

When she first moved to L.A., Sasha bought a computer desk from him. He was preparing to head east to New York City and was clearing out his apartment. Though he was her best friend's younger brother, she didn't know him that well; they'd grown up in different cities. Sasha was surprised at how self-conscious she felt when he arrived, windblown and sexy. He carried the desk in and set it down. He looked proud. Her hair was in a ponytail and she was wearing her worst sweats.

She offered him a beer, and they sat on her couch and shared it. There was so much to catch up on; it had been a few years. He was leaving in a week to start a job on Wall Street. She grabbed a pen and wrote down restaurants and bookstores and museums and bars. When he went to the bathroom, she ran into the bedroom and primped in front of the mirror. There was nothing she could do without being too obvious. It didn't feel right to put on lipstick, a necklace. He walked out of the bathroom and joined her in the bedroom.

"Really cute place," he said.

She'd jumped away from the mirror and stood in the middle of the room.

"Big sister's best friend. It's all so cliché," he said, stepping closer.

Sasha was surprised. "Blake."

"Don't you dare say I'm like your brother," he warned, "because you know I'm not." He was forceful when he kissed her, and she liked it. She freed her hair from its ponytail because it felt right.

He came over every night in the six days before his move. The first two they made out. On the third, they were in bed and as she watched him roll a condom up his penis she was struck by a memory, strong and relentless. Erika still lived in Boston. They were five, maybe six, and Sasha was watching as

Erika's mom changed the baby's diaper. His was the first penis she'd ever seen, rubbery, like a giant thumb. His mother wiped him down and he cooed. Erika wanted to play, but Sasha was too mesmerized to move. She'd never seen anything like it. Now, here it was again, much bigger than a thumb. It was all grown up.

"What?" Blake asked when it was on. "Don't tell me you're having second thoughts."

"I'm not," Sasha said, taking it in her hand, the latex snug and textured. A smile crossed his face, and when she placed him between her legs she thought she heard him coo.

~ ~ ~

Sasha brought her journals into the living room and continued reading while *Dateline* aired in the background. Her journals were dramatic and overwritten. She cringed through most of the pages—this one not talking to that one, crushes on professors ("I will kill myself if he doesn't call on me in class tomorrow"), two muggings, a harsh New York winter, summers home ("Boston is the most provincial city in America"), a fight with her mother over the phone, good restaurants, loneliness. It was all there, scrawled in black and blue ink.

There were also joyful moments captured on the page—the beginning of Sasha's interest in education, pages and pages of musings on love, the start of seeing her parents as adults, her decision to enroll in a master's program. Ultimately she was pleased with her diligent journals, which allowed her to trace the map of her life. She realized that she hadn't written an entry in months, so she found the latest one and picked up where it left off.

Where to begin? If I don't write now, I'll put it off and then I'll never be able to look back and see, in writing, the twist and dip my life has taken. Well, it turns out I'm pregnant, and not your regular have-sex-without-protection pregnant. No, that would be too normal. Instead, Dr. R. thinks my pregnancy is the product of a lazy sperm. Yes, you read it right. Lazicum spermatozoa. *What the fuck? I haven't even thought about the growing creature I have in my body—no, I'm too busy getting blood samples from ex-lovers. I can't even believe I'm writing this. I'm not ready to have a baby. I was barely ready to be an aunt to Erika's kid. And now I'm not even* talking *to Erika! (That's another story, which will hopefully be cleared up by my next entry.) I keep wanting to look for the "whys" of this whole ordeal, but I don't even have time to think about that. I guess that's a good thing. If ever before I've felt chaotic in my life, nothing compares to this.*

Sasha slammed the book shut. Writing wasn't helping; it was only stirring up more confusion. Her phone rang and she let it go to voice mail. It rang again, and she thought about picking up but ultimately didn't. Tomorrow would be show number four in season number two of *Please Pass the Salter*. How she yearned for it to be a typical Sunday night, but no matter how hard she wished, it wouldn't come true.

When Sasha stretched, her shirt lifted. She put a hand on her belly and drummed her fingers. She pushed her hand into her skin. Was it her imagination or did it feel solid? She leaned over and grabbed her date book, which was bursting at the seams. Monday at nine she was due at Dr. Rusmeuth's; at ten she was due in the writers' room. Her phone rang again, and this time she picked up.

"Is this the three-time-award-winning Sasha Salter?" It was Pam.

"No, it's the two-time-award-winning Sasha Salter."

"Don't tell me you haven't heard."

She hadn't.

"No one's called you?" Pam pressed.

"No! I just got home," she lied. "Maybe I have messages?"

"Well, don't listen to them. Let me be the first to congratulate you. *Please Pass the Salter* just won the Pulcinella Award for the best children's show in the world! The *world,* Sasha! And the ceremony is in Italy. Next month. Are you dying?"

Dying? No. Pregnant? Yes. "I'm speechless!" Sasha said. Call waiting sounded. She ignored it, understanding now that all these calls were about the award.

"And that's not all," Pam said.

"More?"

"*TV Guide* is coming to shoot us this week. Are you sitting down? For. The. Cover!"

She'd never heard Pam so giddy. Not even for the Daytime Emmy.

"We rule!" Pam said. "We're going out for drinks after work tomorrow."

Sasha still had her date book on her lap. She glanced down at it. Monday was full of appointments and meetings. She looked at one square earlier: Sunday. Today. It read "Coffee with Sean." She should have written "Coffee and blood with Sean."

"Wait," Sasha said. "It's Sunday. How do we know all this on a Sunday?"

"It's Monday in Rome, my dear. They just announced it an hour ago. I can't believe I'm the first to tell you."

"I know," Sasha said. "This is all so . . ." She was going to say "overwhelming" but settled on "fabulous."

"Fabulous," Pam repeated.

~ ~ ~

At work the next day, things weren't so fabulous. A *National Enquirer* was on the writers' table, with Michael Jackson, white and noseless, on its front page with a small, corner insert of Sasha exiting Cedars-Sinai Medical Center. In the picture, she was looking down at her feet. The small headline above it read "Not So Funny: Kids' Comedy Creator Rushed to Emergency Room." Inside, there was a fuzzy picture of Sasha hugging Sean, as they were saying goodbye just yesterday. The caption underneath read, "Sasha Salter hugs boyfriend after hearing bad news." There was a paragraph below, quoting "sources" who claimed that Sasha had been rushed to the hospital for an undisclosed illness and they didn't know how it would affect her show, *Please Won't You Pass the Salter,* which, of course, was not the proper name.

Sasha had just run into the room to grab a pen. It was still early, and the others weren't in yet. The paper was on the table in front of Pam's regular seat. She had no idea who put it there. It wasn't rare to have reading materials in the room—they were often inspired by newspaper articles, various magazines, and the like—but a *National Enquirer*? With Sasha on the front? She snatched it up and tucked it under her arm as she made her way back to her dressing room.

~ ~ ~

Earlier that morning at Dr. Rusmeuth's office, Sasha was finally feeling better about things. He'd lavished her with praise. He'd already received two faxes, one from a hospital in Boston and the other from Cedars-Sinai: Randy and Sean. When Sasha announced that she had never, in fact, had sex with Oren, the doctor clapped. "Wonderful," he said. His energy was electric. Sasha could actually sense his neurons and transmitters igniting. It made her feel a part of something special.

"Dr. Banks wants to come to one of our meetings," he told her. "I was thinking on Wednesday?"

Wednesdays were hard. "I don't know," Sasha said, though she realized she could sneak out at lunch again. Dr. Rusmeuth leaned forward and called out past Sasha, "Hon? Could you get Klara Banks on the phone for me?"

From the receptionist station came a muted "Okay."

Sasha found it odd that a man in his forties would call his receptionist "hon." She imagined that an old-school doctor in his seventies might speak that way. Maybe his looks were deceiving. Maybe Dr. Rusmeuth was a young-looking fifty. Still, it was a characteristic she noted and filed away among the growing clutter in her brain.

"I said I don't know about Friday," Sasha repeated.

"We'll see what Klara's schedule is like," he said.

Dr. Rusmeuth pulled open a drawer and took out a yellow steno pad like the ones Melanie used. "Let's talk about birth control," he said, fishing for a pen. "What are you using?"

"Nothing right now," she said. "Like I told you."

"Let me rephrase that," he said. "What *have* you used?"

Sasha closed her eyes and took a moment before spilling more of her sexual history to a virtual stranger. "I've tried a lot," she said, launching into it. "The Pill, a diaphragm, condoms. I used the sponge in college, spermicide—alone and with the sponge. But I guess mostly the Pill and condoms. I mean, I don't use condoms, you know, they do. The guys. Men. Whatever."

Rusmeuth was scribbling on his pad. "Do you remember what you used with which partner?" he asked, hopeful. He opened her file and looked it over. "For example, Sean Avery."

"Condoms and the Pill."

"Can you remember the brands?" he asked.

"The Pill was Nordette," she said. "I can't remember condom brands, if that's what you mean. Probably Trojans." Suddenly Sasha was struck with a horrible thought. She blurted it out. "You don't think there's a condom in me?" Her foot started tapping wildly. How could there be? Wouldn't she feel it? Wouldn't Dr. Banks have found it during an exam? What if it had lodged high in her body?

Rusmeuth swiveled in his chair. "That would be highly unusual."

"But isn't this whole thing highly unusual?" She was disgusted by the vision of a condom wrapped around her organs. She tried her best to think of happy things—kittens and puppies and rainbows—but everything that popped into her head came wrapped in an old condom.

They continued playing match-the-birth-control-to-the-lover, but Sasha wasn't great at the game. She was doing her best, and Rusmeuth, busy scribbling down everything she said, barely lifted his head.

"Wednesday's perfect for Dr. Banks," MaryAnne called out.

It was two against one, and Sasha didn't have the energy to fight her case. She threw up her hands in a gesture of "I surrender." When she stood to leave, the chair fell backward, but she didn't reach down to pick it up.

~ ~ ~

Back at the office, a knock on the door forced Sasha out of her thoughts. When she opened the door, Melanie and Fritz were standing—their postures unusually erect, as though they'd just come from a yoga class. Did they even know each other?

"Good morning," Sasha said, still standing in the doorway.

Melanie and Fritz looked at each other.

"Did you guys have a good we—"

Fritz interrupted. "We need to talk to you." He pushed past Sasha into the room. Melanie followed. The *Enquirer* was on the green couch, faceup. Fritz walked right toward it. "We're worried about you," he said, lifting the tabloid and sitting in its place. Melanie sat next to him and extracted another copy from her backpack. She held it up so that both she and Fritz and their papers were in the same positions.

Sasha was still at the door. She decided to close it and walk toward them. Seeing her little corner photo on both papers made her shake her head in disbelief. "Who cares!" she said. "Unbelievable." She sat on the coffee table, facing them.

"Melanie came to me," Fritz said.

"I didn't know who else I could trust."

"And she said she was worried about you. She said—"

"Ever since we went to the doctor," Melanie interrupted, "you've been acting all—"

"Weird," they both said in unison.

"Don't be mad at her," Fritz added. "Don't punish her for being brave."

Brave? How was Melanie brave? Nosy. Pushy. Invasive, maybe. Sasha snatched the paper from Melanie and held it facing them, as though she were about to begin story time. She pointed to the corner photo.

"This is me exiting Cedars-Sinai," she said. She opened the paper and found the article. "And this is my ex-boyfriend Sean." She spoke in a slow, controlled manner. "He gave blood yesterday and wanted me to go with him."

Melanie and Fritz didn't look convinced.

"On a Sunday?" Melanie asked.

"On a Sunday," Sasha said, and then added, "We're facing a huge blood shortage. The bank is always open."

Melanie dug in her backpack and fished for her tools—the steno pad and pen.

"Will you two be donating blood, I hope?" Sasha asked.

"Oh, I'd faint," Melanie said.

"I'll think about it," Fritz said.

Melanie scrawled a few lines worth of notes on her pad.

"Any more questions?" Sasha asked.

The two sat there in silence. Finally, Fritz raised his hand. Sasha nodded for him to speak.

"So you're okay?" he asked. "No doctor connection, not sick, everything's fine? Just hanging out with your ex as he gave blood?"

"That's right," Sasha said in a saccharine tone.

"Did you give blood?" Melanie asked.

Sasha nodded and watched as Melanie glanced at her arm. Shit. No bruise, no Band-Aid. Sasha suddenly distracted them with wild hand movements.

"Wasn't the show amazing this weekend?"

"It was so much fun seeing it on TV," Melanie said, falling into the trap.

"I looked fat," Fritz said.

"You did not." Melanie poked him with her pen. He grabbed the pen and flung it across the room. It was funny, but it didn't warrant Melanie's and Fritz's uproarious laughter. Sasha stood up to get the pen, and when she threw it back it hit the wall and left a blue mark.

twelve

It was incredible to Sasha how many people read the *National Enquirer*. She fielded calls on her cell phone throughout the morning until she decided to record an outgoing message: "Hi. You've reached my cell phone. If you're calling about the *Enquirer,* please don't worry. I was just donating blood." She actually started believing her story. Later in the day, she switched it again when Pam suggested that people who may not have seen it in the first place might now be interested in buying the trashy rag. Sasha agreed but also remembered that the "trashy rag" had been smack in front of Pam's chair earlier that morning.

There were very few times in Sasha's life when she felt that she was going under. Now was one of them. If she continued at this pace—the lies, the planting of evidence, the blood and tissue collection—she would surely go crazy. She already didn't feel right, and it was more than the fact that she was pregnant. She didn't feel right in the head. She felt noisy when she yearned for quiet. She was in the writers' room and things were loud, but she was disconnected from her surroundings. Sticking to her routine wasn't helping, and she realized that the only thing that would save her, at least temporarily, would be to take some time off from work. But how? And why? Now that the story had been printed in the *Enquirer,* people would really think something was wrong, and she'd already worked so hard to prove otherwise.

The writers were talking about incorporating animated interstitials between the sketches. There was a technology that one of them really liked where the computer animated actual people and their movements. He thought that might be an interesting way to go. Another writer suggested animating the tail end of a segment, or maybe both the very beginning and the tail end. Someone else suggested creating a whole new set of recurring characters, like the Simpsons when they were just interstitials. Everyone's eyes brightened at the thought of a spin-off.

After the meeting, Sasha stayed behind with Pam. "I'm thinking I need a break," she said in a convincing tone.

Pam was writing some ideas on the giant whiteboard. "Now?"

"Not right this second." This was so hard for Sasha. Her need for a break would upset so many variables. "Maybe next week." She had heard quite a few stories of difficult actors who shut down a production because they had a headache, or they had broken up with their latest love interest, or they claimed they weren't making enough money. She was now in an industry of enablers; what was so wrong with acting the part every now and then? It only seemed to impress people.

Pam laughed. "You want us to go on hiatus next week?"

"Would that be a possibility?"

Pam stopped writing and covered her pen. "You would tell me if something was seriously wrong, right?" she asked.

Sasha had to think quickly. "It's everything," she said. "It's the *Enquirer* and just . . . the show and the hours and the article that's being written. . . ."

"Melanie?" Pam asked.

Sasha nodded and made up a white lie. "And my parents are coming to town and I'm feeling really tanked creatively and . . ." She had successfully roused a batch of tears. "Is taking a break at all possible? I'm coming to you first."

Pam sat back down and slid her chair close to Sasha's. "Didn't I tell you when we first started that your life was going to change? Remember? I said 'Sasha Salter, your life is about to change.' "

Sasha remembered. But the changes Pam was talking about were manageable, exciting even.

"We all know good stress is just as upsetting as bad stress," Pam said.

Great. Sasha had both. "So do you think the network would go for it? I know it's asking a lot."

"Girl, this is your show. Without you, none of us would be here. I've always told you to wear that more. Don't ask if it's okay. Tell them."

The mere thought of this made her shudder.

~ ~ ~

Sasha and Jordan met for lunch at Victor's deli because Sasha was craving eggs and it was close to the studio. Jordan showed up late, looking disheveled and oddly sexy. He was carrying something, and as he approached Sasha noticed that it was the *National Enquirer*.

"I've seen it," she said as he slid into the booth beside her.

He rested it facedown on the table. A Kool cigarettes ad stared back at them. "I didn't know," he said.

"Was that the frantic need to see me?" she asked, now realizing that it was.

"Can't a guy just want to spend time with his best friend?" he asked, picking up the menu.

"Your hair—" she started.

"It's wet," Jordan said. "I just took a shower at Echo's."

"Showering together!"

Jordan shifted in the vinyl booth. "What's good here?" he asked.

"Anything breakfast."

"But it's lunch."

The waiter approached and slid a plate of lox, eggs, and onions over to Sasha.

"You ordered already?"

"I couldn't wait," she said. And then added, "Cravings."

During lunch, Sasha tried over and over again to get details on Jordan and Echo's burgeoning romance. He was slow to give up much of anything until she reminded him that he knew almost every detail of all of her relationships. The least he could do was share something, anything, about this one. Echo was in her early twenties, he started, and Sasha immediately rolled her eyes.

"That's why I don't tell you," he said.

"But early twenties?"

Jordan threw up his arms in a gesture of "Forget it."

"Sorry," Sasha said. "Go on. And tell me sex stories since I haven't had any in a while."

"Yeah, you've had consequences without the sex," Jordan said, nodding in disbelief.

His meal came—a sausage omelet—and he started with a

few details: the first kiss (which happened within the first hour on the first night of the first date); the first sleepover, which didn't include actual sex but hours and hours of fooling around. And then a sly smile crossed his face as he slipped into vagaries. "It's nice," he said. "It's fun. We click."

Sasha loved the normalcy of their lunch and appreciated how necessary little moments like this were, in light of the bigger situation. Jordan told her about a few interviews he'd lined up at some video-game companies. He admitted that he was on the brink of quitting the promotional company, with or without a job lined up.

Sasha glanced over at the *Enquirer* lying on the table. "I've got to save that," she said, reaching for it.

Jordan slapped her hand and held it. "Are you sure? Because we can throw it away and be done with it."

"No. I need it." She reached for the paper and slid it over to her side of the table. She opened her bag and dropped it in.

"So how many more phone calls to go?" he asked, stabbing the omelet with his fork.

"Four," she said, feeling daunted. "But I'm gonna fly to Tucson this weekend and talk to Javed in person."

"That's an expensive task."

Sasha shrugged. "I can afford it."

"Does he know you're coming?"

"He will."

Clearly, Jordan didn't approve of the plan. He looked at her with a near squint.

"Shut up," she said, though he hadn't said anything.

"You're not going alone, are you?"

"Why? You coming?"

Jordan shook his head in an emphatic no.

Suddenly, having Jordan along didn't sound so bad.

"C'mon. You can finally see where I spent two whole years of my life. You can meet Javed. Don't you want to meet the Indian who broke my heart?"

"Wasn't it the other way around?"

"The heart that broke my Indian?"

When the check came, they both reached for it. In the end Sasha let him pay, and she could tell that it made him feel good.

"Come with me," she said as they were heading out the door. "I'm serious. I'll pay for everything."

"If you really need me, I will."

"I do," she said.

"Then I'm there."

She was filled with gratitude.

~ ~ ~

There was a palpable frantic energy the next day at work. People were running this way and that. Suddenly Sasha remembered that *TV Guide* was coming to photograph them. She headed into her dressing room to brush her teeth. Fritz and Melanie were eating on the floor, picnic style.

"Hi," Fritz said casually. "I hope you don't mind. They're using my dressing room for the *TV Guide* interviews—don't ask me why."

Sasha headed into the bathroom and started brushing her teeth, erasing the taste of lunch.

"You're not mad, are you?" Fritz asked.

"No," Sasha lied.

She heard Melanie whisper, "She's mad."

"The photographer is really cute," Fritz said. "I think you'll like him."

The photographer *was* really cute. He approached Sasha on

the stage, a large camera around his neck, the lens sticking out like an erection.

"Sasha Salter?" he asked, looking sideways at her.

"Yes," she said, alarmed by the size of the lens.

"I'm Scott. I'll be doing the shoot today."

Sasha pointed to his camera. "I figured."

"Congratulations on all your awards and stuff," he said.

How did he know? "Oh, thanks! Yeah. Thanks."

"We'll be doing some group shots, and then I'd like some solo shots of you. Have you ever posed before?"

Sasha laughed. "Professionally? No."

"Oh, but personally you have?" Scott said, smiling.

Sasha could feel herself blush, but she kept on the subject. "Fun with Polaroids," she said, shrugging her shoulders.

The truth was, Javed had had a waterproof, throw-away camera and one night they had taken it into the bath with them. Sasha took most of the pictures—close-ups of Javed's eye, billows of bubbles, her own pedicured foot. The sexiest picture was of both of them, but it was from the neck up and if it weren't for the bubbles they might have been in a Jacuzzi.

Scott's mouth formed into what looked like a snarl as he concentrated on his camera, but he never emitted a sound. His mouth reminded her of Elvis Presley's, and she suddenly wanted more than anything to kiss him.

"I'm looking forward to this kiss," he said. Or had he said *shoot*? She wasn't sure. She hoped he said kiss. What a perfect blunder.

After everyone had been primped by hair and makeup, they were ushered onto the set—Pam, Fritz, Sarah, Ross, Matt, the extras, the director—and posed as though they were the debate team in the yearbook.

"Ya'll look so serious," Scott said. "This is entertainment, folks. Entertain me!"

Everyone brightened. Sasha looked around Scott and saw Melanie, who was urging everyone else to smile. This pissed her off.

"Your show should be called *Please Pass the Smiles*," Scott said, and naturally this made everyone laugh. "Everyone fake-smile," Scott said, and they did. "Everyone surprise-smile." Sasha raised her eyebrows, feigning surprise. She was having a blast. She couldn't wait for her solo shoot. Suddenly, being pregnant from a lazy sperm didn't seem so dire. Suddenly, Erika's not speaking to her seemed pointless. Suddenly, creating a show and doing a *TV Guide* shoot seemed important and necessary and marvelous. She reveled in it—her white teeth, her long hair, her glowing face.

"Beautiful," Scott said. "Beautiful."

thirteen

Sasha sat next to Dr. Banks on the couch in Dr. Rusmeuth's office. He was at his desk, barely visible behind piles of papers and a giant, seemingly outdated computer. She couldn't help feeling that she was in the principal's office, being reprimanded for something. At one time, that would have seemed terrifying. Now, however, she wished that were the case.

"At ten weeks I'd like us to do a CVS," Rusmeuth said.

"CVS?" Sasha knew CVS only as a pharmacy.

"Chorionic villus sampling," Dr. Banks explained. "That's when we'll be able to get tissue samples from the fetus and match it to the father."

"Oh, already?"

They both nodded. Dr. Rusmeuth suddenly looked concerned. This bothered Sasha. "What?" she asked.

"There are a lot of decisions to make after we find out. I don't want you to rush into anything, though," he said.

Here he was again, dancing around the topic: abortion. It's not as if this was happening to her when she was thirty-five and her options would be clearer—she would most likely opt to keep a lazy-sperm baby. She knew that fertility faded, like a forgotten dream, with age, though she was also aware of at least three women in their early to mid-forties who had recently given birth. Still, she was twenty-seven and not even in a relationship—why would she want a child now? And the child of one of her ex-boyfriends at that? Just the thought of a *crib* in her woodsy apartment felt so foreign, so wrong to her. What did she know about babies? Entertaining children, yes. Raising a baby? No, no, no!

"There are other options we can talk about," Dr. Rusmeuth said, clearing his throat. Dr. Banks looked at him sweetly and then at Sasha. He pressed a button on his phone.

"MaryAnne? Could you come in here now?"

Why did he always include the front-desk lady in her very personal situation? Sasha wondered. Wasn't she supposed to simply answer phones and deal with billing? Dr. Rusmeuth rubbed his hands together and looked toward his office door. Dr. Banks followed his gaze, and suddenly the three of them were staring at the door. When it opened, MaryAnne seemed alarmed at the six eyes gazing her way.

"Good morning, everyone," she said.

Everyone responded in unison, like schoolchildren. "Good morning."

"Sit," Dr. Rusmeuth suggested.

MaryAnne pulled a chair right up next to Dr. Rusmeuth, and then she did something that, in Sasha's eyes, was shocking: she took his hand. Sasha kept telling herself not to look, but inevitably her eyes kept dropping down to their hands. Dr. Rusmeuth's thumb rolled around MaryAnne's knuckles. She glanced over at Dr. Banks, who was gazing placidly at them. Dr. Rusmeuth finally spoke.

"Sasha, MaryAnne and I have been trying for years to get pregnant."

"Are you married?" Sasha asked, not because only married couples could have kids but because she'd thought he was the doctor and she was the front-desk lady, end of story. Apparently not. Apparently that was only the beginning.

"It's ironic, isn't it," MaryAnne said.

That wasn't an answer to her question. Sasha turned to Dr. Banks, who was twirling a strand of hair with her finger. "Are they—"

"They are," Dr. Banks said.

She didn't know why it bothered her so much.

"We'd like to make a proposition," he continued. "We'd like to adopt your baby if you're not interested in keeping it." MaryAnne nodded enthusiastically.

Sasha just stared.

"Go on, Ira," Dr. Banks encouraged.

He did. "We are very excited by the possibility that you may be carrying the first product of *Lazicum spermatozoa.* We think you're bright—"

MaryAnne interrupted, "And beautiful. And talented."

"And we feel that it's our responsibility to volunteer to care for this child if your only other option is termination." He lowered his head as he said the word.

Sasha realized that he meant well, but at nine weeks she still felt completely disconnected from this creature growing inside her. There were still so many unanswered questions, still people to tell, decisions to make. How was it fair that, after all the years of safe sex she'd practiced with various men in order *not* to get pregnant, she was indeed pregnant by one of them?

They were exes because the relationships hadn't worked out, not because she wanted to carry one of them's child. How could she go through with the pain of birth, huffing and puffing and pushing and bleeding and tearing, only to give up the child? And give him or her up to Dr. Rusmeuth and MaryAnne—this strange doctor and his front-desk wife? She told herself not to be mad at Dr. Rusmeuth, not to burst into tears, not to stand up and leave. This left her with few options, so she chose silence.

"Sasha," Dr. Banks started, touching her hand to Sasha's knee.

Sasha what? she thought.

"Is she okay?" MaryAnne asked her husband.

"She's overwhelmed," Sasha answered, not meaning to be sarcastic.

"We normally do the CVS between ten and twelve weeks," Dr. Banks explained gently. "We'd like to do it at ten in this case, which for you means next week. That way we'll have answers sooner rather than later, and that way options might become clearer to you once you know who the father is, et cetera."

"I'd also be very interested in examining the father," Dr. Rusmeuth said. "That is, if you choose to tell him and if he chooses to be examined. We would pay for his expenses if he wasn't from here, and, of course, this would all take place under the strictest confidence."

"Have you been able to see that therapist I referred you to?" Dr. Banks asked.

"No," Sasha said. "No, I haven't."

Dr. Banks nodded and pressed her lips together. "I think she'd be very helpful," she said.

"I've been busy at work and with this."

"I know." And that's all she said.

~ ~ ~

Lewis Adler, the executive at the network, was too busy for a face-to-face meeting, so his assistant offered a conference call. Sasha was skeptical. It would be hard to plead her case without using body language, but she'd have to manage.

Sasha, Pam, and Sarah took their seats in the writers' room and stared at the triangular black phone in the middle of the table.

"He's gonna challenge it," Pam cautioned. "But just don't back down."

"We're here to help," Sarah said.

The call came late, and when it did the assistant warned that Adler was on his cell. If the call got lost, she'd return it. "Lewis?" she said. "You're on with Sasha and Pam."

"And Sarah!" Sarah called out.

"I understand a photo shoot took place today," he said. "Sorry I missed it. I heard it was a success."

The women rolled their eyes. No one knew what to say. Sarah finally spoke. "We had some fun," she said. "You'll see when the issue comes out."

There was more awkward silence. This time Pam tried to break it. "How have you been enjoying the show?"

Adler's assistant broke in. "We've lost him," she said. "Can we return?"

When he came back, he sounded curt. "So what can I do for you, ladies?" The term made Sasha cringe.

"Mr. Adler," she began. "I wanted to talk to you about possibly pushing back the schedule." There. She'd said it. More silence. "Did we lose you again, Mr. Adler?"

"Pushing back the schedule?" Adler broke out into boisterous laughter and then grew serious. "It's absolutely impossible," he said.

Sasha looked toward Pam with pleading eyes, but Pam waved for her to continue. "Well, actually, I'm under the impression that nothing's *impossible,*" Sasha said. "If someone had told me a year ago that I'd be hosting a children's show, I'd have thought that *impossible*. But not anymore."

"Your point, Sasha?" he asked over the static.

She thought she had him. She'd have to dig deeper.

"My point is . . ." What was her point? "I need a week off. That's it. I need a week off. It's the simple truth."

"That's not as simple as you think," he said. "You know the old cliché 'Time is money'? That's no cliché."

Pam flashed her middle finger at the phone.

Lewis Adler continued. "Imagine, Sasha, if all my stars and producers and writers on all my shows needed a week off." There were a few beats of silence. "I shudder to think."

"But the chances of that happening at the same time are impossible," Sasha said.

"Are what?" Adler asked.

"Impo—" She caught herself before she finished.

"I thought that word didn't exist in your vocabulary."

Their verbal sparring continued for another fifteen minutes. Pam and Sarah gestured at the phone, but they never chipped in. They never helped. It was Sasha flying solo. She had the distinct feeling that Adler liked to hear himself speak. Instead of saying "No" and leaving it at that, he pushed and argued and spoke in circles until Sasha couldn't stand it anymore. Was that how people got their way? By exhausting other people? It was clear that he wasn't going to budge, but it was also clear that he wanted to assert his power, to make sure Sasha knew her place in the pecking order. Finally, Sasha told him she had to go and he said it was a pleasure talking to her, though he couldn't help her. Before he hung up, he told his assistant to pencil her in for lunch in the next few weeks. Sasha said she'd call the assistant back when she had her date book nearby, even though it was on her lap.

"What a putz," Sarah said.

"Putz," Pam repeated.

Sasha couldn't hold it in. "You guys could have helped."

They looked at each other.

"I—"

"You seemed like—"

"I needed help," Sasha said again, trying not to let her desperation show. Still, saying it felt better than she could imagine.

"We'll figure something out," Sarah said, gazing hard at the table, as if she might be in the process of figuring it out right then.

"What if you took Monday through Wednesday off and just came in Thursday and Friday?" Pam suggested. "We could send you e-mails to keep you posted on sketches and stuff." She looked to Sarah for approval.

Sarah nodded. "I guess that's possible."

"I mean, you'll be around, right? You'll just be running around with your parents. It's not like you're flying off to Brazil or in the throes of a torrid affair, right?"

"I wish!" Sasha said, though soon she would be flying off to Tucson to visit an ex–torrid affair. Monday through Wednesday was feasible. She could go to Tucson over the weekend and then have the CVS procedure on Monday and use Tuesday and Wednesday to rest. It was a tight squeeze, but it could potentially work.

"Well?" Sarah asked.

"I guess it could work."

"So you're happy?" Pam asked.

"Satisfied," Sasha said.

"That's a step in the right direction."

fourteen

Sasha loved the smell of home. Her apartment was surrounded by two eucalyptus trees that gave off a scent that was woodsy, sharp, and spicy, and she reveled in the fragrance. Today had been a day of baby steps, and as she walked into her home she felt a small sense of accomplishment. She dropped her date book on the coffee table in the living room and picked up the phone to check messages.

There was one new message and it was from Erika. She was cold and curt at first, announcing who it was and saying they hadn't spoken in a while. Then she warmed up. She apologized for abandoning Sasha at such a crossroads in her life. Her mom had made her realize that now wasn't an appropriate time to hold a grudge. Her mom? That meant that she knew about Sasha sleeping with Blake *and* about Sasha's pregnancy. There would soon come a time when Sasha would have to tell her own parents about everything that was going on, and she didn't like that notion at all.

Sasha hung up the phone and picked it up again to make a call, but there was no dial tone. "Hello?" she asked.

"Hello," said a voice. A man's.

"Hello?"

"Well, hello again," the voice said.

Sasha stayed silent. The male voice broke the silence. "It's Scott! Is this Sasha?"

"It is." She didn't know any Scotts.

"I'm in the darkroom watching your image float to life."

Of course. Scott the photographer with the erect lens.

"That's poetic," she said, smiling as she sat down on the couch.

"Photography *is* poetry," he said. "If it's done right."

"How'd you get my number?"

"A poet always knows."

"C'mon."

"One of your producers gave me a cast and crew sheet. I said I needed it for name spellings. I'm good, right?"

"S-a-s-h-a."

"S-a-l-t-e-r. Let's have dinner," he suggested. "D-i-n-n-e-r."

Cute Elvis Presley Mouth wanted to have dinner with her? "I was just about to order in." She didn't mean to imply that he should come over.

"Great," he said. "I'll join you."

"No, no," Sasha said. "Let's go out."

"I live up behind the Whisky," he said. "And you?"

"Laurel Canyon," she said, delighted that they were practically neighbors.

"Do you eat meat?" he asked.

"I eat meat," she said.

"I know a great grill-your-own-food place down on La Cienega."

"Gyu-Kaku," she said. "I love it."

"You know it?"

"Of course."

"I just love that you eat meat," he said. "So many L.A. girls don't touch the stuff. 'I'm a vegan,' " he said in a mock-girlie voice.

She ate meat, but she couldn't drink. Oh, well. She'd cross that bridge when she got there.

"Meet there or I pick you up?" he asked.

Sasha considered it. "Meet there." She loved their phone chemistry, but what if he was a creepy kind of date and she had to escape?

"I'm not insulted," he said. "It's smart for a woman to have her own escape vehicle."

She laughed.

"Now call your best friend and have her call your cell phone in an hour. If you're having a bad time, she'll be your out."

She loved this guy, but she wondered why, after a two-year dry spell, a spell more arid than the Sahara, he had popped into her life now? Why couldn't she have met him last year, when the only complication was her busy work schedule? Was this even allowed—being pregnant with one guy's baby while lusting after another?

~ ~ ~

On the ten-minute drive over to the restaurant, she called Erika, hoping to get her machine and leave a message. Erika answered.

"Hi, stranger," she said, recognizing the number from caller ID. "I love you."

"I love you, too," Sasha responded.

"It's just really weird that you fucked my brother."

Sasha couldn't believe her ears. Erika never talked like that. "I know," she said. "And I'm sorry we never told you. It was stupid." It wasn't stupid at all. It was fun, and she didn't regret it.

"I'm over it," Erika said. Sasha knew this wasn't true. Erika held on to things. It's just who she was. "Anyway, how are *you,* my pregnant best friend?"

Sasha didn't think this was the time to tell her that she was en route to meet a date. "I'm hanging in there," she said. "I've got two samples already and—"

"Three," Erika said. "Blake's submitting whatever you need."

"You told him?"

"Aren't you glad? Another one down, and you didn't even have to make the call."

She understood why Erika thought she'd be glad, but she wasn't. Making those calls was part of facing her reality—her surreality.

"Hello?" Erika said to the silence.

"I'm here," Sasha said. "Honestly? When I—"

"You're seriously mad at me?" Erika asked. Her voice was tinged with anger.

"No, I'm just saying that when I—"

"Because I'm the one who should be mad at you, and I've worked very hard not to be."

Now wasn't the time to berate Erika for doing what she considered a favor, she knew that. She wondered how that conversation took place. She could just picture the expression on Blake's face—confused and intense. "What did he say?" Sasha asked.

"Well, if you must know, it was a really uncomfortable conversation."

"I can imagine," Sasha said. "I've had it a few times now."

"Why don't you come over and I'll tell you about it in person," Erika said. "Are you heading home from work?"

"Yeah," Sasha lied. "I'm really tired, though. Maybe we can talk about it another time?"

"Fine," Erika said, sounding insulted.

Sasha changed the subject. "Next week I have to get a CVS. Do you know what that is?"

"Of course. And I'm coming with you."

"Oh, that's okay. That's really sweet but—"

"Believe me, you're gonna need someone there, and I bet a million dollars Jordan won't want the task. When are you scheduled for it?"

"Next Monday."

"You're twelve weeks already?"

"No, they're doing it at ten."

Silence.

"Hello?"

"And this is the only option?" Erika asked.

"They're doing what they have to do. I'm not thrilled about it."

"It's your body," Erika warned. "Just remember that."

~ ~ ~

Scott was sitting outside the restaurant as Sasha approached. She felt a little shaken by her conversation with Erika, but as soon as she saw him she relaxed.

"We meet again," he said. He stood up and gave her a warm hug.

"I'm starving," she said. It was hard looking at him, he was so cute. She forced herself. They made eye contact and she felt a *zing*. It had been so long since she'd felt a *zing*. "I almost didn't recognize you without the camera around your neck."

"It's like my extra appendage," he said, grinning.

They entered the restaurant to a flurry of greetings, and a tall, beautiful woman escorted them to their seats.

"Well, if it isn't Ms. Sasha Salter!" Sasha looked to her right and there was Fritz at a corner table. Melanie was sitting beside him.

"Oh! You scared me!" Sasha said.

Scott recognized them, too, as he'd taken their pictures only yesterday. "Hey, man," he said.

The hostess was ahead of them, but when she saw that they were conversing she backtracked. "You want to sit with your friends?" she asked Scott.

"Yeah, sit with us," Melanie said.

Sasha tried to give Scott a look that said, "No, please, no," but since they didn't know each other at all he interpreted it as "Yes, please, yes" and motioned for her to scoot in first. She was heartbroken.

"What are you doing here?" she asked them. They each had beers in front of them but no food.

"I love this place," Fritz said. "I think you introduced it to me. I wanted Mel to try it."

"So far, so good," Melanie said, raising her beer to her lips.

"Two words," Scott said. "Harami beef."

Melanie wrinkled her nose. "I'm a vegan," she said.

Scott and Sasha laughed.

"What?" Melanie said.

"Nothing," Sasha said. "We were just talking about vegans earlier."

The waitress came by with plates of vegetables.

"Harami beef," Sasha started. "Shrimp garlic, miso scallops, unagi bibimba—"

"What's that?" Melanie asked.

"Eel," Scott said.

"Eeeew!"

Sasha suddenly wondered if she could eat eel. She knew there were all sorts of dietary rules around pregnancy. "Never mind—no unagi," she said.

"Why?" Scott asked. "I love that stuff. Yes, unagi," he told the waitress, who was erasing and writing. "And two Asahis," he added.

"Oh, just one," Sasha said.

"Okay, one. We'll share."

Over dinner, Melanie tried three times to glean information for her interview. Finally, Sasha had to ask her to stop. She was trying to have a relaxing meal.

"I just thought fate sent you here for a reason," Melanie said. "Thought I'd try to get what I could while I had you."

Sasha wondered why fate *had* sent them there, with Fritz and Melanie. She couldn't figure out if they were dating or not. Sure, they were on the same side of the booth, but she still didn't pick up a sexual vibe from them. Maybe it was wishful thinking on her part. Meanwhile, as Fritz was telling a story about a misguided college prank, underneath the table Scott put his hand on Sasha's thigh and squeezed. Was he trying to say "Help, this is so boring," or was it something else? He inched his hand higher and then rubbed it back and forth. Sasha suddenly had the feeling that he wasn't even listening to

Fritz's story. She lowered her hand and touched his, and they sat that way for the rest of dinner.

When the bill came, Sasha pulled out her wallet, but Scott motioned for her to put it away.

"I've got it for us," he said.

"And I've got it for us," Fritz said to Melanie.

"You didn't touch your beer," Melanie pointed out. Everyone looked at the amber liquid.

"Oh, yeah," Sasha said. "You want it?"

Melanie reached over and gulped it down.

Sasha was full, and she felt the first bubbles of indigestion as she stood up. Fritz, Melanie, and Scott had valet-parked, while Sasha had found a spot on the street.

"I'll walk you to your car," Scott offered. And after they said their goodbyes and see-ya-tomorrows Scott gently guided her around the corner, leaned her against the outside wall of the restaurant, and kissed her. "I've been wanting to do that all night," he said.

Sasha was over the moon. Those thick, pouty lips felt like heaven against her own. She pulled him in for more. When was the last time she kissed someone? She couldn't even remember.

He pulled away. "I think she likes it," he said.

Sasha laughed. "So remind me . . . who are you?"

"I'm the camera guy."

"Oh, right. Thanks for dinner," she said.

"My pleasure."

"Sorry about the company."

"That Melanie girl is a pill," he said.

"Thank you!" Sasha said.

"You're welcome!" He laughed.

"Sometimes I think I'm the only one who thinks that."

"You know what?" he said, brushing a strand of her hair behind her ear. "Can we move this conversation into your car?"

"Definitely. As long as we don't talk about Melanie anymore."

They ran to the car, which had a city of Beverly Hills ticket slapped on the windshield. They were momentarily distracted by reading parking signs and the ticket, but then they were in her car, steaming up the windows. It was incredible to Sasha how alive she suddenly felt. When was the last time she had made out in a car? It felt so desperate and wonderful.

"I love your car," Scott said, coming up for air. "But I know some other, more comfortable spots where we can do this."

"Yeah?" Sasha asked. "I have to be at work at seven. Wednesdays usually aren't late nights for me."

"Yeah?" Scott asked.

Why should she deny herself the simple pleasure of kissing someone? Why did she feel an overpowering need to say "Good night, see you soon." Kissing led to fucking, that's why. Not always, but in this situation probably so. Plus, she didn't know this guy. Plus, what if kissing led to something else? Like some horrible disease? She couldn't trust her body anymore; it had clung to an errant sperm for God knows how long.

"I'm not going to sleep with you, Scott," she said.

"I'm not gonna sleep with you either," he said. "We *are* just kissing, right?"

Now she was embarrassed, assuming that he wanted to sleep with her—moving ahead of the situation at hand. Why couldn't she just *be*—in the front seat of her pearl-green Saab. "Just be," she told herself.

"Can we just be here a little longer?" she asked. Why was

she asking his permission? "Let's just be here a little longer," she corrected herself.

He smiled and leaned back in the seat. "How much is your ticket for?"

"Who cares?" she said, inching over to his side. "Whatever it is, it's worth it."

fifteen

Sasha couldn't help herself, but she practically skipped into work the next day. It was seven in the morning, and she was vibrant and friendly. The writers' session didn't start until nine, but she had things to take care of—fan mail to answer, memos to read. Melanie wouldn't be in until nine either, so she set about sending an e-mail to Javed.

She was succinct and to the point. She was coming to Arizona for business and would like to see him. It was imperative that she see him. She wouldn't book her flight until she knew he'd be there. She sent it to both his home and work e-mail. Next she logged on to Southwest's Web site and scanned the fares. Los Angeles to Tucson was merely thirty-nine dollars. She reserved two seats. Then she opened a new window and searched for nice hotels in the area.

While she was waiting for a page to load, she decided to do a Google search on chorionic villus sampling, the test she was due for next week. What came up surprised her. She pored over link after link of explanations. No wonder Erika was concerned. This was a risky test. The chances of miscarriage were one in a hundred. She played out the various scenarios in her head. She could have the test, find the father, and lose the baby. She could have the test, find the father, and keep the baby. She could opt out of the test, stop searching for the father, and tell Dr. Banks she wanted an abortion.

As she sat there driving herself crazy with possibilities, she got an e-mail response from Javed: "Business in Tucson? I thought you'd gone Hollywood. Would love to see you. Call upon your arrival. J." Her heart leaped. The trip was officially on.

Melanie came in at eight. Sasha couldn't understand why. She looked different: her hair was blown straight. It was surprisingly chic.

"Nice hair," Sasha said.

Melanie smiled. "I spent, like, an hour doing it."

"It's worth it," Sasha said.

"So, I saw some sparks flying with a certain someone last night."

Sasha closed all the windows on her laptop and put it to sleep. "With you and Fritz?" she asked.

Melanie's face spilled into a vibrant red. It kept getting darker and darker. Sasha was sorry she'd said anything.

"I meant with you and Scott."

"He's nice," Sasha said. "I mean Scott, not Fritz." She corrected herself. "I mean Fritz is great, too."

"I know," Melanie said.

Sasha couldn't bear to see the poor girl blush anymore, so she changed the subject. "Tomorrow's your last day," she said, adding a pouty face for effect.

"I know." Melanie pouty-faced back.

"So when will I get to see the article?" she asked.

"I'm not sure. I think it'll be in the August issue."

"August?"

"Yeah."

"But when do I get to see a draft?"

"You don't," Melanie said, spreading her belongings out on the coffee table.

"Wait, so something's being written about me, sight unseen?"

Melanie laughed. "Believe me, it's hardly sight unseen. It goes through, like, a million editors before it makes it to print."

Sasha hadn't even thought to ask for article approval. She didn't even know if this was something she *could* ask for.

"Don't worry your pretty little head," Melanie said.

Sasha was disgusted by her attitude, but Melanie was going to be there for only one more day, so she held her tongue and went to call Jordan from her cell phone in the quiet of the conference room.

He answered in a whisper.

"Wake up!" she said, aware that she was being obnoxious.

"What time is it?" he asked, groggy.

Sasha heard someone in the background say, "Eight fifteen."

"Oh!" Sasha said. "Overnight guest?"

"Why are you calling me so early?"

"Who is it?" the voice asked. Clearly, it belonged to Echo. Why was she so nosy?

"It's my friend Sasha Salter," Jordan said.

"Oh."

"We're set for Tucson. Friday to Sunday," Sasha said.

She was met with silence.

"Hello?"

"I'm here."

"You're still coming, right?" she asked.

"I'll get back to you on that," Jordan said.

What was he doing? "But you said you'd come with me."

"Um. Can I call you back?"

"Jordan."

"Okay, I'll call you back," and he hung up. Just like that.

When Sasha sulked into her office, Melanie was on her computer.

"Hope you don't mind," she said. "I'm just checking my e-mail."

Sasha walked over and shut the laptop. "Yes, I do mind, Melanie."

"I was checking my e-mail."

"You leave your papers scattered all over my space, and not once have I looked at any of them. Why? Because it's your private property and it would be rude of me to invade that."

Melanie looked like a wounded bird. "I'm really sorry," she said.

Sasha was tired of her apologies, her dull face, her pushy personality. She unplugged her computer and took it with her into the empty writers' room.

sixteen

Sasha and Jordan were on the plane, in the backward seats, because Jordan thought it would be fun. In their ten years of friendship, they had never flown together, and now that they were in the process of doing it Sasha couldn't stop calling attention to it.

"I would never have guessed that you're a backward-seat guy," she said.

"Hey, if there's a backward seat on a plane, I'm all over it."

They were in midair, munching on pretzels, speaking above the hum of the engine. Upon boarding, Sasha was greeted delightedly by the flight attendant. She asked for an autograph for her niece, and Sasha complied. Now that same flight attendant kept pausing at their row whenever she had a lull in her work schedule.

"So what brings you two out to Tucson?" she asked.

Jordan and Sasha looked at each other, but neither answered.

"Ya'll headed there on vacation?"

"Sort of," Sasha finally said.

The flight attendant laughed. "Ya'll headed out there on a 'sort of' vacation?"

Sasha was thankful the flight was only an hour.

"We're working on a project together," Jordan said. "We have to be in Tucson for our project."

"Ya'll married?" she asked.

They both answered "No" at the same time, in the same tone.

"We've been friends for ten years," Jordan clarified.

Sasha stood up to use the bathroom, and when she returned the flight attendant was in her seat. Jordan was in the middle of a complicated story, and Sasha had to clear her throat for him to stop. She finally reclaimed her seat as the flight attendant collected trash.

"Jesus," she said.

"What? Me or her?"

"Both of you," Sasha said.

"What?" Jordan said. She saw him tuck something into his jeans pocket.

"Is that her phone number?" Sasha asked a bit too loudly.

He shrugged her away as she tried to reach in and retrieve it.

"Would you stop?" he said, laughing now.

"Give it to me," she said, digging into his pocket. Their seatmates, the ones facing forward, peered over their magazines. When she finally dug her fingers in, she pulled out a red pretzel wrapper.

"Seriously?" she asked. "That's all that's in there?"

Jordan rolled his eyes.

"Why are you putting trash in your pocket?"

Jordan ignored her and instead looked out the window. Sasha followed his gaze. The sun was setting and it cast the most perfect, powerful light against the wisps of clouds. It looked like white gold, and being above the clouds felt so freeing and safe.

"Isn't it amazing being alive?" she asked. She was suddenly filled with gratitude and peace.

Jordan smiled and nodded, still looking out the window. "I was just thinking the same thing."

~ ~ ~

The hotel was much fancier than the Web site had portrayed. The landscaping was incredible, with pools, cactuses, and pebbles strewn around the grounds.

"Nice digs," Jordan said, soaking it all in.

"Aren't you glad you decided to escort me?"

"Did I have a choice?"

Sasha felt bruised by the response, but before she could say anything Jordan put his arm around her and gave her a squeeze. "Kidding," he said, though she knew he wasn't.

They checked in and headed up to their room. It had two double beds, as she'd requested, and a view of the garden at the side of the property. The mountains stood stalwart in the distance. Sasha forgot how spectacular the terrain was. When she'd lived there, she'd practically taken it for granted. What a pretty environment to have studied in, she thought, unpacking her carry-on bag. She hung a blue sundress on a hanger and took her cosmetics bag into the bathroom. She splashed cold water on her face and ran a brush through her hair. She looked tired.

Back in the room, Jordan was checking out the TV. Sasha plugged in her cell phone to recharge it.

"I guess I'll call him now. Ideally, I'd like to see him tomorrow. We can have dinner tonight or something. 'Kay?"

Jordan was busy selecting choice video games from the TV screen. He quickly figured out how it worked and began thumbing the joystick and shooting up asteroids.

When Sasha reached Javed, he was just leaving campus even though it was eight at night. She wondered if he was in the throes of another affair. He explained that he was trying to finish all his grading at work so that his home space would be just that—home space. It was jarring, hearing his voice. He sounded sturdy and confident. Just as she was thinking this, he told her it was good to hear her voice, that *she* sounded happy and confident. Leave it to them to think the same things about each other. They made plans to meet the following night for dinner, though she didn't know how she would eat, between the daunting task of telling him her news and the reality that she still had feelings for him. As they were chatting, her call waiting sounded and he suggested that they continue their conversation in person. When she clicked over, she found Scott on the other line, inviting her out for drinks.

"I'm in Tucson!" she said, laughing. She explained that she was visiting an old friend from graduate school. Jordan looked at her, and she lifted her finger to indicate "I'll explain . . ."

"What about tomorrow night?" he asked.

"I'm here all weekend."

"Oh, that sucks," he said.

"Sure does," she said. "But don't worry, I'm coming back."

"Have dinner with me on Sunday?" he asked. "It's not as romantic as Friday or Saturday, but if that's all you can offer I'll take it."

Sasha twirled a piece of hair around her finger. "Can we confirm that night? I don't want to come home exhausted and—"

"We'll play it by ear. Dinner maybe Sunday." And then, "I miss you."

"I miss you, too," she said, even though she didn't really.

Now Jordan gave an exaggerated "Who is that?" face, and Sasha lifted her finger again. He rolled his eyes.

"Bye," she said to Scott, and flipped her phone closed.

~ ~ ~

At dinner, in the opulent hotel restaurant, Sasha brought Jordan up to speed on the past few days and, most important, on Scott. Earlier, the waiter had brought a bottle of Pinot Noir over to the table, compliments of the restaurant manager whose three kids were fans of *Please Pass the Salter.* She couldn't drink, so Jordan had his glass, then her glass, and was now pouring himself a third.

"Well, how's that going to work?" he asked, referring to Scott.

"I don't know," she said, because she didn't.

Jordan swirled his glass. The wine sloshed around.

"Are you nervous about tomorrow?" he asked.

"I am. But I'm also really looking forward to seeing him," she said. Of all her exes, this Indian professor was the one that meant the most to her.

"So did you really need me here?" Jordan asked, sipping the wine.

"Of course I did!" Sasha said, surprised. "My God, of course!"

They dined first on exotic salads, then Sasha had a light

lemon risotto while Jordan opted for a filet mignon. The food was worth the high price. Afterward, they feasted on a cheese plate with stinky, creamy, thick cheeses.

"So I have a question," Sasha said, popping a grape into her mouth. Even though she hadn't so much as tasted the wine, the decadent meal and the lush surroundings made her feel open and relaxed. Jordan looked at her. "What the fuck am I going to do about my situation?"

"The baby situation?"

"Is there another one?"

"Are you ready to have a baby?"

"No. But I always thought if I got into this the *normal* way I'd have the right to choose."

"You do have the right to choose."

"But now that I'm in it, it's not exactly an easy decision."

"But it's one that has to be made." Jordan spread some Havarti on a thin cracker. "Have you thought about adoption?"

"I've thought about every alternative under the sun," she said. "All I do is think about what to do. And this baby is getting bigger as we speak."

Jordan chewed his cheese and cracker and pointed to his own stomach. "After tonight's dinner, this baby is getting bigger, too."

Sasha laughed. "What would you do?" she said, nodding in the direction of his stomach. "Seriously."

Jordan took a thoughtful pause. "If I was pregnant from a lazy sperm, by Jordan Kerr," he said, pretending to read an essay. "If I was pregnant from a lazy sperm, and I was a girl"—he switched back to his regular voice—"I'd probably keep it."

"Really?" Sasha said.

"I think I'm at that place in my life. Financially, things are fine. It's just the girl that's missing."

"What about Echo?"

"Would you stop it with her already?"

Sasha slumped in her chair.

"What's your instinct telling you?" Jordan asked, pouring himself the last drops of Pinot.

"That you're an alcoholic."

"Ha."

"My mind's not quiet enough to hear my instinct."

Jordan swallowed the remaining wine in one gulp.

"And I guess it kind of depends on who the fucking sperm belongs to," she said. "If it's Javed, yeah, I guess I'd keep it. I mean, a brilliant mind like that? Of course I'd want that for my kid."

"Suppose it's Sean's?"

"Abort," she said too quickly. "No, that's mean. I don't know."

"Maybe you can make a list of all the guys and their good and bad qualities."

"John Robinson. Bad quality: he's dead."

"I still can't get over that," Jordan said, shaking his head.

"I sent his parents a sympathy card. I almost wrote what was going on. I know he had a brother and ultimately I could get samples from him, but I decided not to. I just have to hope it's not his."

"Then again, if it is his, don't you think his parents have a right to know their grandchild?"

"Oh, my God," Sasha said. "I didn't even think about that."

"Or you could abort before you know who the father is."

"I could," she said. "That I've thought about."

"Was it weird that I just said that?"

"Please," she said, indicating that it wasn't. "This doctor . . . God, now *this* is gonna sound weird."

"Try me."

"He's made it very clear that he and his wife are interested in adopting."

"Well, there you go!" Jordan said, as though this was the easy answer, the perfect solution.

"This whole arena is his specialty. Basically, the kid would be a by-product of everything he's been trying to prove."

"But that's good, right?"

"What if he treated the kid like some sort of trophy? What if he traveled around lecturing about *Lazicum spermatozoa* with *my* kid?"

"Don't all parents treat their kids like some sort of trophy?"

"And, like, what . . . I give birth and then go back to work? I mean, do I even have a relationship with this kid?" The bill came, and they both reached for it. Sasha flicked his hand away. "This whole weekend is my treat," she said. "Seriously. I couldn't do it without you." She paid with her credit card.

~ ~ ~

Back in the room, Sasha kicked off her shoes and jumped into the bed near the window.

"So tired," she said. She closed her eyes for an instant, and when she opened them Jordan was sitting at the foot of her bed. "Aren't you gonna play video games or something?" she asked.

Jordan scootched closer to her. "Do we have to wake up at eight to watch your show?" he asked, kicking off his shoes.

Sasha looked at him as he positioned himself next to her and closed his eyes.

"Do we?" he asked.

"Is it such a chore?"

Jordan rolled over toward Sasha. "Just asking," he said. "Don't get your tail feathers in a snitch."

Before she could respond, Jordan was kissing her.

seventeen

Jordan's tongue was deep in Sasha's mouth, and she didn't know what to do. It wasn't that she didn't enjoy the act of kissing; it was just that a ten-year tension of never having kissed suddenly felt sacred and, now, broken. She could taste his red wine, his breath. His mouth was warm and wet. It wasn't that it was unpleasant; it was just that it was Jordan. When she pulled back, he opened his eyes, his mouth still agape.

"Jordan—"

He closed his mouth and rolled onto his back.

"Really? Now?"

He rubbed his face. There was such an awkward silence. She hoped for a cricket to chirp or a car alarm to sound—something to break the excruciating silence. She didn't know what else to say.

Jordan sat up and leaned against the headboard. "Do you know how hard it's been for me?" he asked, crossing his legs.

She was shocked by his question. For him? Hard for him? "I have to sit with you and make lists of people you've slept with. Sean and Blake and Matt and John and Javed, and I'm thinking, What's wrong with me? Am I so bad that I'm the only one who's not on the fucking list? I mean literally the 'fucking list.' " He brought his arms over his chest and crossed them, too. His stomach rumbled. It sounded like thunder in the distance.

"The *list*?" Sasha said, her eyes widening. "The list is seven people long, Jordan. Not exactly gigantic. What's your list? Probably twice that, three times that—no, four times that. How is my list suddenly—"

"You're not hearing me," he said.

He was sulking. On her bed. About not having slept with her. Was this really happening? "I hear you," Sasha said. "I get it. But sleeping with someone and loving someone . . . they're not always connected."

She looked at him, but he was now facing his own bed.

"I know. I'm just saying . . . I'm here with you while you're inter . . . inner-acting with someone you love . . . loved . . . whatever. A lot. And I'm, like, why the fuck did he get to sleep with her and I didn't?"

She couldn't believe the words coming out of his mouth. Clearly they were fueled by the bottle of wine, but it wasn't as if they were coming out of thin air.

"I'm sorry," he said, looking at her. "I'm being selfish."

He wasn't being selfish. He was being honest. Up until this point their friendship had been a pressure cooker. Here, tonight, in a hotel room in Tucson, Arizona, it had exploded.

All she could think to say was, "What about Echo?"

"What about Echo," he answered. "She's a twenty-two-year-old baby." He was just saying that because she had said it the other day.

"No. Twenty-two's not a baby. I was in graduate school at—"

"I don't love Echo. The sex isn't even that great, by the way. I mean, she's twenty-two . . . shouldn't she *want* to have sex a little more than once a week?"

"I guess."

Jordan looked at her, his blue eyes probing. She stared back. She was caught in his gaze. There was so much to him. Sasha fought the urge to look away, and soon she didn't even feel the urge; nor did she feel the need to break the moment with a joke, a comment. She had never looked at him this way and she was absorbed in his many emotions, which floated by. She stared at him until he looked like a stranger. Who was this stranger in her bed? He finally slipped down onto his back and closed his eyes. Within minutes, he was snoring.

Sasha stood up and headed into the bathroom to brush her teeth. She changed into her pajamas and considered sleeping in Jordan's bed, but instead crawled back into her own. In the middle of the night, she awoke to Jordan's arm draped around her. So now not only was she pregnant from a lazy sperm, she was in bed with her best friend. She exhaled and fell back asleep.

When she woke up in the morning, the TV was on and Jordan had returned to his bed. Her show was halfway through. Had she really slept in? She looked at the digital clock next to her bed. Yep. She had.

"Morning," Jordan said.

"Morning," Sasha said without looking at him. Did they

have to continue where they'd left off last night? "How's your hangover?"

He groaned.

There was an unquestionable awkwardness in the air. Only ten hours ago his tongue was in her mouth. Now it seemed the cat had his tongue. Sasha flipped over and watched a few minutes of the show. Then she flipped to her stomach and practically willed herself back to sleep. Magically, it worked and soon she was dreaming of ribbons—streams of ribbons hanging from a pole, like a Maypole only not. She was entwined in the colors as she weaved through them. The colors were electric, blues, pinks, yellows, and they felt soft on her skin. When she awoke again, it was almost ten and Jordan was in the shower.

Sasha picked up her date book and extracted a piece of paper with the numbers of various Matt Millers in the New York area. There were eleven of them. She started at the top. A woman answered the first call, and when Sasha asked for Matt she put a child on. Sasha hung up as soon as he said, "Hello." The second number gave her someone's voice mail. It sounded as if it could be a man in his late twenties, so she decided to leave a message. "Hi, I'm looking for the Matt Miller who attended NYU and graduated in '99. If this is you, could you please call me back?" She gave her cell-phone number and only her first name.

As she was dialing the third number, Jordan came out of the shower with only a towel wrapped around his waist. He looked small and sad, his wet hair matted to his head, little droplets of water rolling down his arms.

"I'm in search of Matt Miller," she told him as she dialed. She lifted the piece of paper to show the number of Matts she had to weed through. Jordan came closer and looked at the paper. He smelled fresh.

"I have Matt's number," he said.

"You do?"

"Aren't you on his band's list?"

"I have no idea what you're talking about." She wished he would get dressed.

"He's in some band, and they play pretty regularly."

"In L.A.?"

"New York."

"You're on his list?" Why was Jordan on her ex-boyfriend's list? Furthermore, what kind of band was Matt Miller in? He was a stockbroker, last she'd heard.

"I have it at home. I'll give it to you when we get back."

"Great," she said, relieved not to have to make any more calls.

Matt had still been with his high-school girlfriend when Sasha met him their freshman year at NYU. Not only did they live in the same dorm, they were in Spanish class together. They struggled through conjugations and translations, and spoke only in Spanish when they ate together in the cafeteria. He was mild and kind. Funny but not hilarious. Decent. Their sophomore year Matt broke up with his high-school sweetheart and switched to French.

"Me haces falta," Sasha called out to him one day when she passed him in the hall. He had since moved to another dorm, too, and she hadn't seen much of him lately. She really did miss him.

"Me haces falta," he said back. She wasn't sure if he was correcting her or saying he missed her, too.

It was that casual exchange that planted the relationship

seed. He's so sweet, she thought to herself as she walked to class. So nice.

Matt and Sasha were together from their sophomore year until the summer before senior year. Having a steady boyfriend made Sasha feel sophisticated. By their first summer together, they'd met each other's families. They planned on living together their junior year, but Matt won a dorm lottery that landed him a room in Alumni Hall. Ultimately, it had ended up being more cost-effective for both of them to stay in the dorms.

Matt was the first boyfriend with whom she'd had a continuous sexual relationship. Before Matt, her sex life had plodded along in fits and starts. Then it wasn't a big deal. It's not that sex took a backseat, but it was integrated in a way that it hadn't been before. It didn't define their relationship; it was merely a component. Inspired by Erika, Sasha went on the Pill when her friendship with Matt turned romantic. She kept the monthly packet beside her bed and popped the little pink tablets every morning. She tried not to think about the effect they were having on her—the way they reorganized her system. Even so, they mostly had sex with a condom, but by their second year together they were trying it without. When Sasha didn't get pregnant, they tried it again. It was a whole other feeling being latex-free—one she could definitely get used to.

They were young, so their crises revolved around semesters abroad, Christmas breaks, and schoolwork. They were dubbed "the married couple," and Sasha wondered what she was missing out on, having this person around all the time. A Matt baby would be intelligent and grounded. Perhaps a bit dull.

"Now," she said to Jordan, "I just have to find Billy Lambert to see if I can locate Chad."

"Can't help you with that one," he said, grabbing some clothes from his bag.

They spent the day wandering around the University of Arizona campus. It was a Saturday, so it wasn't buzzing the way it would be on a weekday. She toured Jordan around her old haunts—the library, the student union, the classroom in the psychology building where she was a teacher's assistant, the education building. She could see through his eyes that these were just brick buildings, but to her they stored so many memories. It was a lifetime ago that Sasha had roamed the campus, loving the feeling of being in the hot desert sun, being out West. At the time, graduate school had consumed her life, between papers and presentations, classes taken and taught, research, romance. Being here now, it seemed like an oasis. The calm before the storm.

Signs for an upcoming football game lined the quad. Jordan looked one over. "You were a Wildcat?" he asked.

Sasha mock-rolled a set of pom-poms. "Gimme a 'W,' " she shouted. Some students looked at her as they walked past.

She took him to Fourth Avenue for lunch—the hippie enclave, dotted with stores, beggars, restaurants, and bars. They sat in the squat chairs at the Casbah teahouse. Sasha had spent a lot of her time there during graduate school, grading papers, writing papers, drinking tea. Today a strong wind blew through and the colorful drapes bustled in the gust. A busboy, one she remembered from a few years ago, came out and fixed an umbrella that had been tossed around. When he saw her, he smiled. "Hey, you," he said. Sasha waved back, wondering if he really remembered her.

They drove the rental car on the scenic route back to the hotel. Sasha thought about her own journey out from Boston to Tucson so many years ago now. As she'd approached the

Southwest, she thought the desert landscape looked hand-delivered from a movie set: the mountains, cactuses, and tumbleweeds. She saw profiles in all the rocks—a man with a big nose making a sad face, a lady with pursed lips. The cactuses amazed her. She would later learn to identify them—prickly pear, hedgehog, giant saguaro—but on her first drive they were "hand giving the finger," "man standing at attention," "penis." Now, driving down River Road, the cactuses looked like spectators cheering on the sidelines. Sasha hit the accelerator, honked the horn, and let out a "Woo hoo!" much to Jordan's surprise. Their day touring Tucson ended back at the hotel, where Jordan announced that he was going to soak in the hot tub. They parted ways.

Up in the room, preparing to meet Javed, Sasha threw on her blue sundress and settled on a coral-colored gloss she'd "borrowed" from the makeup department. She smacked her lips together. She was ready to go.

~ ~ ~

Javed was one of those unlucky men who were assaulted by migraines. Sasha had never seen anything like it, and was seduced by the power that was handed to her whenever he was rendered powerless. He always knew when one was approaching, because his energy increased, and it was not just a caffeinated buzz; it was more of a total jolt. He could be anywhere—in front of a classroom, driving home, making love—when suddenly he would catapult into warp speed—talking, driving, or fucking too fast. He'd have a good fifteen or twenty minutes of hyperspeed, and then the headache would land, as he put it, and he'd be out for at least twelve hours. The lights had to be off and all noise had to be hushed. The medicine helped, but the headaches would only slip from severe to terrible, which really didn't make a difference when you were in the throes of pain.

These were, oddly, fond memories for Sasha: sitting in silence in his room, in the dark, holding his hand—watching the crease in his forehead slowly and eventually unfurl. She would stare at his face and hands and torso and try to comprehend how someone so peaceful could be in such pain, and, further, how his pain could bring her such peace.

When Javed arrived at the restaurant, Sasha could tell immediately that he was in pain. He looked piqued and unsteady. He walked in so hurriedly that he passed Sasha, who was standing by the front door. He walked briskly into the dining area and looked around from left to right. When he turned, he spotted her. He shook his head and approached.

"Hi. Here," Sasha said, waving her right hand.

Javed bent down to kiss her just as she turned her face to kiss him. They ended up rubbing cheeks and blowing air kisses.

"Is this some sort of Eskimo thing?" she asked.

"No, this is," he said, rubbing noses with her.

Sasha thought back to their first-ever conversation. It was early in the semester, and one of the second-year graduates had held a welcome party at his house for faculty and students. Theirs was a small department, and in the few weeks Sasha had been in Arizona she'd already met the whole group. At the party she found herself in conversation not with her classmates but with Javed Rimposhe, her Developmental Psychology professor. He told her that he championed her acceptance into the program as soon as he read her essay, which was about being an only child. He was fascinated, not just because she was able to use it as a springboard for why she would thrive in the academic atmosphere but because he came from a family of seven and couldn't fathom an upbringing as quiet and attentive as hers.

Over the course of the night, they'd moved from the porch to the kitchen to the living room and back to the porch. Their conversation connected like a perfect game of dominoes. It was September in Tucson, and it was hot. The crushed ice in the daiquiris cooled Sasha and she slurped down more than she intended. Javed morphed from a stoic, mannered professor into a handsome, laid-back guy. So he was forty-two, recently separated, her professor. At that moment he represented her new life, her intellectual endeavors, her future.

"I must get going," he said, suddenly standing up.

"Awww," Sasha said. "Who am I going to talk to?"

"Mingle with your classmates," he said. "They're a very nice group this year." She stood and considered hugging him. He leaned in to kiss her cheek, but she tripped on his foot and their lips met instead. Hers were cold from daiquiri ice, and his were warm from the Arizona heat.

After a four-month flirtation, glances in class, conversations in the mailroom that included five people, then four, three, and finally just the two of them, after department potluck dinners where they sat next to each other bumping knees and finishing each other's sentences, they finally slept together. It was fantastic. Sasha attributed it to the four-month buildup, their physical and intellectual connection, and, of course, the taboo nature of the relationship.

The day after they slept together, Sasha followed him to his office after class. She wanted to know how they would progress from there. She'd never done anything like it before. She hoped he hadn't either, but since he was older and perhaps wiser she thought he might have some insight.

Instead, Sasha found herself having a conversation about

John Bowlby. Javed wanted to know what she thought about his lecture on Bowlby's attachment theory. Sasha had studied him at NYU and had strong opinions. Javed's office door was slightly ajar. They were standing next to each other. He was wearing sunglasses and a black leather jacket. She wanted to touch his face. Instead, she rambled on about Bowlby. She respected his theory that the attachments infants form with their caregivers become the basis for establishing patterns of attachment for the rest of their lives, but she also had questions: How did they know that infant attachment wasn't merely a function of feeding? Could the theory be used cross-culturally? Javed appreciated her questions and explained the answers. Their conversation dripped with subtext. At one point, after she leaned in to kiss him, saying, "What about this attachment?" she noticed that he was turned on. His crotch bulged. She stepped in closer and reached down and touched him gently. He cocked his head to the side and smiled. She wished they were in one of their homes, in one of their beds. Sasha took a step back just as the door swung open and a young male student walked in.

"Professor Rimposhe?" he asked. "Can I talk to you about my midterm grade?"

Javed cleared his throat and raised his glasses to the top of his head.

Sasha had worried about his erection, which she thought, stealing a glance at it, looked obvious. She nudged the office wheely chair toward him. "Professor, I'm sure you'd rather sit," she said. "You've been standing all day."

Javed negotiated his way into the chair and crossed his legs. "What's going on, Anthony?" he asked the student.

"Thanks, Professor," Sasha said. "I have no more questions about Bowlby."

"Oh, sorry," the student said. "I didn't mean to interrupt."

"It's okay," Sasha said. "We're done."

Javed lifted his hand to wave. His smile was sly. As Sasha left the office, she could hear Anthony complaining about his essay grade while Javed listened intently.

She remembered that day thinking how challenging their affair would be, never entertaining the thought of falling in love, which she did—the love creeping up on her like rising water. She worried that she would drown in it but instead found herself swimming. Around him, she'd felt light and buoyant and tranquil.

~ ~ ~

When they were finally seated, Javed explained that he wasn't feeling so well. He thought he might have a headache coming on, but it hadn't landed yet and it was unusual for him to feel this off for so long without the headache. Sasha smiled sympathetically and said she understood. He begged her to order a nice wine but warned that he couldn't join her.

"Well, here you are," he said, tearing at a piece of bread. "I wish you'd given me more notice; I'd have invited you to speak in my class. If you do that sort of thing."

"Oh, I would have loved to. This was sort of last-minute, though," she said, not ready to jump into details.

Under the table, Javed crossed his legs and bumped Sasha. "Sorry," he said.

She kicked back. "Sorry," she said.

This was a little game they used to play when they were together—at restaurants, dinner parties, school events. They'd both found it hilarious. Now it felt contrived.

"I really didn't mean to bump you," Javed said.

"I did," Sasha said, and continued looking at the menu.

"So what's your life like?" he asked.

"It's really quite boring."

"Love life boring, too?" he asked.

"It's L.A.," Sasha said. "All those rumors you hear are true."

"Such as . . ."

"It's a really hard place to date," she said, though in the past forty-eight hours she'd kissed two different men. She didn't want to pursue this line of questioning because it was too painful, and she didn't want to hear his answers.

"You must meet interesting people," he said. "C'mon, by now you must have met a movie star, no?"

How could a brilliant professor care about a vapid movie star? "I don't know. You see 'em at restaurants. I've seen Cameron Diaz and what's-her-name, Minnie Driver. Oh, and Jeff Daniels told me he and his kids watched my show. We were in line at the same dry cleaners."

"I don't know who that is."

"That guy in the movie *Dumb and Dumber*."

"There's actually a movie called *Dumb and Dumber*?"

They sat in silence until their salads came. Sasha sprinkled some salt on hers. Lately, she'd been craving salt. She wanted to ease into talking about her pregnancy, but she thought it could wait until the main course.

"So this all worked out for you," Javed said. "This whole California move."

"It did," Sasha said. "And I have you to thank for it."

"I'm not fishing for that," he said.

Their entrées came and then dessert, and there was still no talk of anything. Sasha thought maybe once the waiter cleared the table she'd delve into it, but after the waiter came and left she still couldn't bring herself to have the conversation that needed to be had. She wanted more than anything to go home with Javed and hold his hand in the dark.

"Did your headache land yet?" she asked as they waited for the check.

"I think it dissipated," he said with a smile. "Who needs Imitrex when you've got an evening with Sasha Salter?"

She took this as a sign, of what she wasn't sure, but she reached out her hand and touched his fist, which rested on the table. She covered his smooth brown skin with her own delicate hand. They stayed like this for a bit, until he escaped from under her.

"Well, I've got some news," he said, clearing his throat. His voice suddenly became louder and more pronounced, his posture erect. "I'm getting married. Again."

Sasha retracted her hand and put it on her lap. Under the table, her left foot tapped uncontrollably. "Wow!" she said, and smiled too widely. She was all teeth; she could feel it. "Congratulations."

"Another chance for me to get this marriage thing right. Third time's the charm, I'm hoping."

"That's what they say."

This complicated things. What if the lazy sperm was his? And what if he wanted the baby? Sasha's mind was spinning. What if, what if, what if.

"We met at a conference last year in Texas."

She was dying to know, but she hadn't asked. She looked at him.

"I found Texas to be quite alarming," he said. "Quintessential Americana. The conference was in Austin, but we stayed on and visited Dallas."

Their conversation continued about the state of Texas, not the fiancée, for the next several minutes—the weather, the landscape, the food. It seemed the night was over, and still Sasha managed to elude the real reason for their meet and greet. It suddenly felt too late, but she had come so far.

"I have a question," Sasha said after Javed had given a lengthy soliloquy about tamales. She waved her finger at him and then at herself, and repeated this action. "Us."

"Us," he repeated, mimicking her finger movement.

"Is it just me? Or was it significant for you?"

He stopped wagging. "Why do you choose now to ask?"

"Was I just passing through?" she asked. "In your eyes?"

"Sasha, you remember. I was going through a very hard time four years ago."

"Yes, but that's not my question."

"We were not on the same page," he said. "I was there, but I wasn't *there*. The way you were there."

"And you knew that then?" she asked.

He looked down at his shoes but didn't answer. "Everything's so different now," he finally said, looking up. "Moving forward is such a healing direction."

His last statement confirmed her decision not to tell him. How could she? It would suck his life right back to the painful past. He talked about moving forward as if he had a choice. But she didn't. She had been pulled back by something completely beyond her control. In the end, she would forgo getting samples and telling him her incredible news. If none of the others came back positive, she'd reconsider. But for now this was her decision.

Their hugs were not equal. Javed clung to her, and she very purposely let her body go slack. She touched his back without meaning. They were in the parking lot of the restaurant. She was tired. And thirsty. She hoped the air would be clear when she returned to the hotel room.

~ ~ ~

Jordan was waiting in the lobby, talking to an older couple, when Sasha returned. When he saw her he exclaimed, "There she is!" The couple turned and smiled.

"Your boyfriend was worried about you," the woman said. She reached for her husband's hand.

Earlier, Sasha had noticed signs for a fifty-year high-school reunion being held upstairs in the hotel's atrium, a fancier version of the lobby. She wondered if they were two of the attendees.

"Fay and Joe are here for their reunion," Jordan confirmed.

"Fifty years," Fay said.

"Congratulations," Sasha said. Was attending a reunion worthy of congratulations? Surviving high school certainly was. Surviving in general was, too.

"High-school sweethearts," Joe said, squeezing his wife's hand. Sasha didn't have the energy to hear their story, sweet as it might be.

"They met in geometry," Jordan said.

Sasha nodded and then added, "I always hated math." Everyone looked at her as though she'd declared her distaste for puppies. The couple said goodbye and strolled away.

"Nice to meet you," Jordan called after them.

"Boyfriend?" Sasha said.

"How'd it go tonight?" Jordan asked.

She shook her head.

"You didn't tell him?"

Sasha felt the unmistakable swell of tears forming. "Can we go sit outside?"

The moon was reflected in the pool. Sasha stared at the moving water splicing the light into angles, like an abstract painting.

"Will you tell me why you didn't tell him?" Jordan asked.

She didn't know the answer. The evening was still playing out in her head. She realized it was Javed's mind that she was so attracted to. He had brought out the best in her mind as well. He spoke to her intellect. He conjured her intellect. It had always been there, but he gave it shape and focus. She was ready for it. Eager for it. She gulped it down as though she were parched in the desert. With Javed, it was all about the mind. What was missing was what came from the heart. They shared love, but it wasn't whole. It was fractured, like the moonlight in the pool.

"Do you want to go swimming?" Sasha asked.

Jordan laughed. "No. Not really."

"He doesn't understand things unless they come from here," Sasha said, pointing to her head.

"Hmm," Jordan said. "Sucks to be him."

They sat in silence for a little. The night air was warm and fragrant. Suddenly Jordan stood up.

"I changed my mind," he said, and before she knew it he'd kicked off his shoes and jumped, fully clothed, into the pool. The splash was sloppy. Water doused everything, including her. She laughed and leaned back in the lounge chair.

"It's fucking freezing, but it feels awesome," Jordan said. He reached out for her, but she shook her head. She, too, had changed her mind.

~ ~ ~

The hotel shower had a fierce head, and water pelted Sasha's shoulders in an aggressive, slicing sensation. Her belly, naked and wet, looked as though she had eaten a rich meal, followed by some beers. No one would notice, really. No one who didn't know her body. Her breasts, normally small and unassuming, had begun to swell with pregnancy. Her bras were snug, and she felt immense relief when she removed them for the evening. In the past week she had started wearing a sports bra at night so she wouldn't awake to a throbbing, bruising feeling.

Sasha toweled off and entered the bedroom. Jordan was on his bed, lying on his back, eyes closed, hands resting behind his head. He looked so relaxed, and this was a palpable antidote for the way Sasha was feeling. The TV was on in the background—a barely audible episode of *Dateline.* Jordan's kiss last night, coupled with the utter lack of anything with Javed, suddenly aroused Sasha. Her body had been untouched for years. She remembered reading Sylvia Plath's journals in college and being struck by the entry "Could I die from this? From lack of touch?" She knew what Sylvia meant now, and with her nipples swollen and eager for touch, and her friend's posture, open and receiving, she felt compelled to do something about it. If she thought too much she'd think herself out of it, so she dropped her towel and walked over to Jordan's bed. His eyes were still closed. They opened as soon as she slid her damp body over his. His eyes registered confusion for a moment and then delight.

"Hello," he said.

She adjusted herself to him, hip bone to hip bone. He was on top of the covers, wearing boxers and a white T-shirt. She put her hands on his shoulders, his stayed behind his head, and she started to rock herself gently up and down over him. Her breasts grazed his shirt. Jordan pursed his lips.

"We can't have sex," Sasha said in a voice lower than she'd anticipated. "Not now."

Jordan nodded and groaned and then released his hands and placed them on her behind, helping with her movements. She could feel a significant swell between her legs.

"Feel good?" he asked, rocking with her.

She nodded as her body movements accelerated, and after she'd slipped into a gentle orgasm she rested her head on Jordan's chest, his heart beating loudly in her ear. He wrapped his arms around her back and squeezed. Without looking up, she raised her hands to his face and touched both of his cheeks. She moved them back to his shoulders after a few seconds. As her breath steadied, she could hear the murmur of the television.

"Look at me," Jordan said.

She lifted her head. He had a sheepish smile, so she smiled back. She inched up his body to reach his face and initiated a kiss. It was during the kiss, right before she was going to say "See? I *am* a Wildcat," that she heard Stone Phillips's voice over the speakers.

"A woman becomes pregnant, but she doesn't know who the father is. That's because she hasn't been sexually active in over two years. Isaac Asimov story, or real-life situation?"

"What?" Sasha screamed.

"What?" Jordan asked.

Sasha sat up and turned toward the TV. There was a black silhouette of a pregnant woman.

"Tune in next week as we explore the concept of delayed fertility and *Lazicum spermatozoa*."

Sasha jumped up and stood closer to the TV. She turned away only to retrieve her towel, which was on the floor. "How is this on TV?" She wrapped the towel around her and tucked it in, as though she had just stepped out of the shower.

Jordan was sitting up, looking at the television. "That's weird," he said.

The end credits rolled and they cut to a commercial. Sasha sat on the corner of the bed and looked pleadingly at Jordan. Gone was their warm exchange.

"We don't know it's you," he said.

There was the known, and there was the unknown, and lately they had blurred and become inextricably linked.

eighteen

Their plane was late, and Sasha was going out of her mind at the crowded terminal.

"We don't know it's you," Jordan said for what felt like the fiftieth time.

"Well, I'd like to be hooked up with this other person. My God, I have a fucking soul mate out there? Please let's meet. Who can introduce us?"

"You don't know—"

"It's me, Jordan. It has to be me. Dr. Rusmeuth promised. He swore to me—"

"You'll sue," Jordan said. Another quick fix.

"Oh, I'll sue? I'm trying to keep this quiet, not call attention to it."

"Well, I don't know what you fucking want me to say anymore, so I'm going over there to make a phone call." He pointed to another seating area at a gate nearby.

"Fine," she said.

He walked off, dialing his cell phone.

Sasha took a seat and rummaged through her purse. She extracted her date book and looked up Dr. Banks's number: she had her work number and her home number. Normally, she wouldn't feel comfortable calling a doctor at home, but these were extenuating circumstances. She dialed and the phone rang a few times before a child answered.

"Hello?"

"Hi, is your mom there?" Sasha asked.

"Who may I ask is calling?" the little girl said.

"Sasha Salter."

There was silence on the line.

"Is this Mia?" Sasha asked.

Still silence.

"Mia. Is your mommy there?"

After a few more seconds of silence, Sasha heard the phone drop and the sounds of running footsteps. "Mama!" She heard the trail of Mia's voice. After what seemed an eternity, Dr. Banks finally came to the phone.

"Sasha?" she asked.

"Yes."

"I'm so sorry about that. Is everything all right?"

Sasha explained the scenario in a shaky, hurried voice. "How is this possible?" she asked.

"I don't know," Dr. Banks said. "I'm going to call Dr. Rusmeuth right away. There's a chance it's not you. He works with a lot of unusual cases, and that's just in Los Angeles. I'm sure there are other doctors in other cities and countries who are involved in the same kind of research."

"I'm not happy about this," Sasha warned her. The anger in her voice even surprised her. "Any of this," she added. She could hear Dr. Banks exhale on the other end of the line.

"You've got your CVS tomorrow, is that right?"

"Yes."

"We're going to have answers very soon, Sasha. Just hang on a little longer. Can you do that?"

"I don't know."

"Would you like me to come to the test with you?"

"That's all right. My friend's taking me."

"This is an important week for us," Dr. Banks said. "We're going to get to the bottom of this. If I hear anything from Dr. Rusmeuth, I'll call you."

~ ~ ~

The flight home was turbulent. Jordan read the airline magazine while Sasha filed her nails with the manicure kit she'd taken from the hotel. She was not usually a nail person, but the steady rasp of the file took her mind off the shaking of the plane. They were sitting in the regular seats, and on this flight she felt none of the anticipation of the last. Furthermore, the original mission of the trip had not been accomplished, while another, more ephemeral development had taken place. Neither of them spoke of the night before, and she wondered if they ever would.

They were walking through LAX when Sasha asked Jordan how they were getting home.

"Echo's picking me up. I'm sure she'll give you a ride, too."

"Oh."

Before Sasha could devise other ways—taxi, shuttle, Erika—they were out through the glass doors and onto the street.

"There she is!" Jordan said.

Sasha saw a freckled girl in a white Mini Cooper. As soon as the girl spotted Jordan, she hopped out of her car and ran over. She was bouncy, bubbly, and just plain adorable.

"Welcome wagon!" she said, stretching her arms out for a hug. Jordan complied.

"This is Sasha," he said with a smile.

"Sasha!" Echo leaped into Sasha's arms, too. "I've heard so much about you!"

Sasha returned the hug. "You, too," she said.

Echo was a little pixie. She grabbed their bags, one on each pixie arm, and tossed them in the back of the car. "It's a tight squeeze, but we can all fit."

"I'll drive," Jordan said, cupping his hands for the keys. Echo twirled them on her finger before flinging them to him.

"I'll sit in the back," she suggested.

"No, no, I will," Sasha said.

"I'm not putting a celebrity in the backseat of my car," Echo said with a giggle. Before Sasha could argue, Echo sprang into the back and wiggled herself to the middle of the seat. "First time in my own backseat!" she announced.

Sasha tried to match her enthusiasm with a big smile. With Jordan at the wheel, it felt to Sasha as if they were driving their kid to camp or something. Sasha looked over at Jordan as he maneuvered out of the airport. When he met her gaze, she knew that he was thinking the same thing.

When they arrived at Sasha's place, Echo bounded out of the car and twirled into the driveway. "I love this neighborhood!" she said. She closed her eyes and breathed deep. "What is that? What is that? Eucalyptus!" She was ecstatic, moving quickly into euphoria. "I love eucalyptus!"

Jordan got out and put his hands on Echo's shoulders. He steered her back in the direction of the car. It was a cute, coupley gesture, and it made Sasha sad.

"Thanks for coming, Jordan," Sasha said. "I couldn't have done it without you."

"Done what?" he asked.

"Had an orgasm," she wanted to say, because she knew that's what he wanted her to say. It was their private joke now. Or was it merely a buildup to a joke? Maybe it was just the punch line. Echo stood on the passenger side of her car, waving. "Everything," Sasha finally said.

"Anytime," he said. "I mean it."

"Nice to finally meet you, Echo," Sasha added.

Echo flashed the peace sign before disappearing into the car.

~ ~ ~

It felt as if she'd been gone forever, when really it had been less than forty-eight hours. Her parents were the first message on her machine, just checking in, and Scott was the second. He reminded her that it was Sunday and they had a maybe date. Could she call him to confirm?

No, she couldn't confirm. Sasha refused to lie through yet another dinner. She'd lied the night before with Javed and would have to do it on the phone with her parents. It was too draining. Scott and his erect lens would have to wait—perhaps nine months. Perhaps forever. If there was another date in their future, so be it, but tonight there wouldn't be, and when Sasha came to that realization, she felt immense relief.

Scott, however, wasn't as happy. In fact, he was defensive and belligerent. "I kept the night open," he said more than once. He tried to bully her into changing her mind, and when she refused he made sweeping generalizations about women: "I don't get women in this town. Don't they know a good thing when they see it?" "Women in this town lead men on." Sasha hung up, hoping that the *TV Guide* with her picture on the cover wouldn't arrive on the stands with her wearing a Hitler mustache.

~ ~ ~

Later that night Sasha's cell phone rang an unfamiliar tone, and when she went to answer it she found that she had a text message—a feature she rarely used. It was Jordan sending her Matt Miller's number. They hadn't spoken since their return earlier that day from Tucson. It was Sunday night, the CVS test was the next morning, and she was antsy, nervous, and in the mood to talk.

She'd been thinking about her college boyfriend Matt a lot lately. Their sex life had fizzled toward the middle of their second year together, and by the spring it was nonexistent. They still loved each other and got along fine, but they slept together less and less. Sasha figured it was just a phase and was convinced that their relationship had reached a certain comfort level. It was only when she befriended Mercedes, the Spanish graduate-student T.A., that she realized their dormant sex life might be a sign of something else.

After class one day, at a coffee shop where Mercedes was grading midterms and Sasha was writing an English paper, talk turned to their relationships, and though Sasha didn't feel particularly close to Mercedes, she opened up, telling her T.A. that things with her long-term boyfriend were at a standstill in the bedroom.

Mercedes listened and nodded. *"Juntos pero no revueltos,"* she said knowingly.

Sasha arched an eyebrow. She hadn't learned that one in Spanish class.

"Together without the scrambled," Mercedes said. "Like scrambled eggs," she clarified.

"Juntos pero no revolutios," Sasha repeated.

"Revueltos," Mercedes corrected.

"I love it," Sasha said. "I mean, I don't love that we're living that way, but I love the saying. Will that be on our final?"

"No way," Mercedes said, laughing. "But life is all about the scramble." She wove one hand into the other. "The scramble is good. *Muy importante*. It gets your juices flowing."

Sasha wondered how many other students had talked about juices with their T.A.s.

~ ~ ~

Sitting in her kitchen, she grabbed the phone and dialed the number. The man who picked up sounded older and more confident than Matt; she could tell just from his hello. He explained that Matt was at a gig, and when Sasha identified herself he nearly gasped. "No way!" he said. "We watch your show! You went out with Matty in college."

He didn't have to explain: just by calling him "Matty," he'd told her this was his boyfriend. *Juntos pero no revueltos,* she thought. It now made a little more sense. "Who's this?" she asked anyway.

"Darryl," he said.

"Nice to meet you," she said. "I'm gonna take a leap and ask if you're his . . . partner?"

"Four years next month," he said.

"Four years," Sasha said, wrapping her brain around the idea.

"We're so in love with your show," he said. "Swear to God, not just saying it 'cause you're on the phone. Matty's gonna die that he missed you."

She wondered when Matty had come out and if his "It's not you, it's me" speech so many years ago had actually been true.

"He sings in a punk band," Darryl said. "The Conjugate Surds. It helps him blow off steam from ye ole day job."

Sasha leaned back in the chair and settled into a long conversation with Darryl. He seemed warm and genuine and funny. He worked in publishing, had met Matt at a reading, and had graduated from NYU two years before them. They knew professors in common from the English department. Darryl wanted to know all about Matt's hetero days, and she launched into the memories that had recently come flooding back. She almost forgot the intent of her call until Darryl remarked with delight that he heard the key in the door. They'd talked for so long that Matt was now back home. It was nine-thirty her time, twelve-thirty his. She imagined him thrashing around onstage in a little club downtown. Sunday was the new Friday—that's what Melanie had told her just last week. He was probably exhausted. Maybe she should save her story for another time. But when Matt picked up, immediately apologetic for his years of absence, she could tell that he was wide awake and that she had better launch into it now.

She'd forgotten how kind he was—just the tone of his voice put her at ease. He was steady and even, the perfect person to be with during a disaster. This situation was a disaster of sorts. After ten minutes of pleasantries, Sasha said, "Well, I'll just cut to the chase, I guess."

"I knew this wasn't just a catch-up call," he said.

Sasha asked if he'd ever heard of the term *Lazicum spermatozoa* and of course he hadn't. She told him about Banks, Rusmeuth, the bats, the pending CVS, the DNA. It tumbled out of her for the third, fourth, fifth time. She knew now how to navigate through the awkward silences, the questions, the disbelief. Matt's reaction was similar to the others'—why wouldn't it be?—but he agreed to the blood sample. He'd go to Columbia Presbyterian on his lunch hour. "What are you gonna do, Sash?"

"Just figuring it out day by day," she said.

~ ~ ~

The next morning, Sasha found herself the passenger in yet another car. Erika was driving her to Santa Monica, where she was finally having the chorionic villus sampling. The results of this test would yield answers, and answers would yield decisions, and soon, perhaps, this chapter of her life would end. Or begin. In any case, she was moving forward.

Sasha tried to avoid Erika's questions about Arizona. "It was fine," she said.

"And?" Erika asked.

"And interesting."

"Interesting how?"

Sasha wasn't in the mood to rehash Javed—to admit that she hadn't told him or gotten samples from him, to admit that he'd never loved her. She wasn't in the mood to describe rubbing herself over Jordan's erection or meeting Echo twelve hours later. She wasn't in the mood to tell Erika about the *Dateline* episode that was airing next week, but in light of all the other events this seemed to be the easiest.

"Interesting because on Saturday night we saw a coming attraction for next week's *Dateline*." She glanced over at Erika, who was biting her lower lip.

"We saw it, too," she confessed. "I wasn't going to tell you."

"I'm livid," Sasha said. "Not at you," she clarified.

"Do you think it's you?"

"Of course it's me."

"How did they—" Erika started.

"I don't know. The same way the *Enquirer* found me at the hospital. So many people know now. Just the other week it was only me, Dr. Banks, and Dr. Rusmeuth. Now it's Randy and Sean and you and Jordan and Blake—"

"You're not suggesting my brother has anything to do with this."

"How do I know he didn't tell his girlfriend and she told her sister and she told her nephew, who has a friend at *Dateline*?"

"Because he doesn't have a girlfriend."

"You know what I mean. It's out there. I don't know who knows anymore."

At a red light, Erika put her hand on Sasha's knee and smiled. The gesture was both empathetic and sympathetic.

Sasha continued, "But I know who *doesn't* know. My parents. And shouldn't they really be first on the list?"

"Tricky one," Erika said. "I think it's okay for you to process this on your own before telling them. It's not like you're five."

"If I were five, we'd really have a problem."

~ ~ ~

Sasha filled out the paperwork in the waiting room while Erika got lost in a *US Weekly*.

"I'm sorry, ma'am. Only Sasha can come in at this time," the nurse said when Erika stood up to accompany her.

That didn't stop her. "No, we're together."

They stepped into the examining room and Sasha was surprised and upset to see that the specialist was a man. She had been told that someone named Lauren Evans was doing the procedure and automatically assumed it was a woman. But it was a man: L-O-R-E-N. He was friendly enough. He instructed Sasha to change into a paper gown and put her feet through the stirrups. He looked over at Erika. "When are you due?"

"Three weeks."

He nodded. "My sister-in-law and her partner are having their kids at the same time, too," he said before leaving the room to let Sasha undress.

Sasha was fumbling with the gown when Erika finally figured out what he'd said. "He thinks we're lesbians!"

Sasha laughed. She'd thought he was a woman, he thought she was a lesbian.

"No offense, but *eeew*!" Erika said. At twenty-seven, she still led a relatively sheltered life. Sasha hadn't yet told her about her conversation with Matt and wondered if, when she did, she should divulge all the details.

Dr. Evans returned, and Sasha positioned herself on the table, legs apart, feet in stirrups. Erika stood behind and held her hand while the doctor busied himself with the instruments.

"By the way, my friend Erika wants me to clarify that we're not a couple."

"Sasha!"

"She's my best friend. It's a coincidence that we're both pregnant."

Erika squeezed her hand. Dr. Evans looked up for a moment and smiled. Sasha employed her breathing techniques as she felt a pinch.

"Can you tell the sex from a CVS?" Erika asked. What was she doing? Sasha didn't want to know.

He wheeled over to Sasha. "We could ta—"

"No," Sasha said firmly. "I don't want to know."

"Okay," he and Erika said at the same time.

After the test was over, Sasha felt infused with a manic energy. They'd have the results in between seventy-two hours and a week.

"No sooner?" Sasha asked.

The doctor shook his head. He reiterated how important it was that Sasha take it easy for the next twenty-four hours, and that she call her regular doctor immediately if she experienced any bleeding or cramping.

"You heard him say how important it is to take it easy," Erika warned on the elevator ride down to the garage. "That means no going to work, no dinners out, no running around."

"I heard."

Sasha leaned back in the passenger seat and closed her eyes. She wondered what Jordan was doing, what he and Echo had done last night. Did they have sex? What, if anything, had he told her about their trip? Did Echo sense anything different? Her mind raced through the possibilities, and before she could censor herself she blurted out, "I kind of fooled around with Jordan in Tucson."

They were at a stop sign. Erika slapped the steering wheel with her hand. "I knew it!" she said gleefully.

Sasha opened her eyes. "How?"

"I could tell by the way you were talking about him. This is great. Should I call the wedding planner?"

"C'mon. It doesn't mean—"

"It's a step in the right direction."

In her nervousness about the CVS, Sasha recounted the entire weekend for Erika—from Jordan's drunken kiss, to Javed's dismissiveness, to Sasha's pleasuring herself atop a sleepy Jordan.

"Jeff and I haven't had sex in months," Erika said. "And it's not because I'm not interested. Maybe I should do what you did. Mount him and rub myself all over him." It sounded so forceful when she put it like that. "You go, girl!" she said, slamming her hand on the wheel again.

It felt good to get it off her chest, and as soon as Sasha did she started crying. When Erika looked over, she started crying, too.

"What are you crying about?" Sasha asked.

"What are *you* crying about?" Erika asked.

Neither of them answered.

"Look at us," Erika finally said. "Two pregnant women crying about nothing."

But that wasn't true. Sasha was crying about everything.

nineteen

Erika brought her home, made some tea, tucked her into bed, and headed out. As soon as she left, Sasha kicked off the covers and went into the living room to call Fritz. Being away from work made her edgy. She wanted to know what was happening. A woman answered his phone, and just as Sasha was about to ask for him she realized it was Melanie and quickly hung up. What the hell was she still doing there? Didn't she have an article to write? A job to go to? Didn't the production team on Sasha's show wonder what the little snit was doing hanging out so much? Eating their craft services? She had to find a way to talk to Fritz about it.

Sasha took her mug of tea and sat outside on the front step. In Arizona she'd lived in a boxy, soulless apartment. She'd never imagined that here, in Los Angeles, she'd be nestled in the woods, like a fairy tale. She was rural, five minutes away from urban. She lifted the tea bag out of the mug and placed it next to her on the concrete step. As soon as she did, a kitten emerged, circling and sniffing it. The cat looked only a few months old. It had a pushed-in face and silky gray fur. Animals often roamed the property—deer, coyote, ducks—but she had never seen this kitten before. It was pawing the string of the tea bag, engrossed in the activity.

Sasha had always wanted a cat, but both of her parents were too allergic. The closest she'd come to getting a pet was in kindergarten, when she took home the class rabbit, Peter. From Friday to Sunday night, she had an overwhelming sense of fear. Sure, she fed him carrots and marveled at his pellet poops, but she couldn't wait to return him, worried that he was eating too much, or not drinking enough, or that he'd escape the cage and hop down the stairs and out the front door. She was consumed with bunny nightmares for those three nights, and each time she awoke, terrified, Peter was always sitting innocently in his cage flaring his little nose, staring at her with his beady eyes. Two weekends later, when Scott Forestman took custody of him, he died, attacked by the family dog. Sasha, with the rest of the class, was saddened by the news, but mostly she was relieved that it hadn't happened on her watch.

"Where's your mama?" Sasha now asked in a high-pitched voice. She stuck out a finger for the cat to sniff. It pushed into her with its nose and dropped to its back, all four paws skyward. She cautiously rubbed its little belly. "Where's your mama?" she asked again. The cat rolled and twisted and purred. "Where is your mother?" she called out, louder and more sternly. The cat sprang up and bounded away, leaving Sasha alone and in tears.

~ ~ ~

It was one thirty in L.A., four thirty in the afternoon in New York. Sasha logged on to her computer and tracked down the number of the *Dateline* production office. When she got through to someone, she donned an English accent. It made her feel less nervous. "Hello," she said. "I'm cawling about a segment you're airing next week. The one on *Lazicum spermatozoa.* I've got some information I'd like to share with the producer."

The woman asked for her name and number and promised to pass it on. Sasha gave her name as Lisa, and in an attempt not to reveal anything about herself she rattled off Jordan's phone number. Next she called Jordan to warn him, but there was no answer and no machine. She let it ring seven times. She hung up, thinking about her other pleading calls. "Jordan, I *need* you." So many calls started with those words. Now, thinking about it, Sasha felt ashamed. Theirs was a relationship based on her needs and his meeting them. How could she apologize for years of this behavior? She felt a surge of love for his safety net. She was always jumping in, and he was constantly there to catch her. What had she given him, she wondered, to prompt his confession in Arizona? Or was it merely a case of too much Pinot?

For dinner, Sasha threw together a salad of leftovers from the fridge. She'd felt fine all day. No cramps, no bleeding. She secretly hoped for one or the other—a sign that something was wrong, a decision made for her. So far, however, the fetus clung on, and by now, according to a baby site on the Internet, it resembled a shrimp, with a large head and a small body. There were chat rooms for everything from tender nipples to baby's first kick, but nothing about a lazy sperm wiggling its lazy fucking tail up to her overly accepting egg and finally—after years? a decade?—settling in.

She was already in bed reading when Dr. Banks called. It was only eight, but Sasha was exhausted. Dr. Banks wanted to know how she was feeling and to tell her that Dr. Rusmeuth hadn't yet returned her call. "It's not unusual, though," she added. "He's got a lot on his plate."

"So do I," Sasha said.

"I know," Dr. Banks said.

"Who *is* this Rusmeuth, anyway?" Sasha asked in a tone that sounded as though she were impressed rather than confounded.

"Dr. Rusmeuth is an unconventional thinker," Dr. Banks said. These were the same words she'd used before. "Why? What's going on, Sasha?"

"I just wonder if there's anyone else—"

"You've come so far already," Dr. Banks said. "But if you really want to start with someone new, I'd be happy to do some research and refer you."

More appointments, more stories, more sex talk with strangers, more sneaking out of work. "Thanks," Sasha said. "I'll think about it."

~ ~ ~

That night, her dreams were insignificant. She wanted a sign, a message, some help from her subconscious as to what she should do. The answer was inside her, she knew it, but so far it had refused to emerge.

On Tuesday morning, Jordan called to tell her that a producer from *Dateline* had called him looking for a Lisa.

"What'd you say?" Sasha asked.

"I told him Lisa wasn't available and got the number where Lisa could call him back."

"I'm Lisa," Sasha said.

"I know," Jordan said. "The fake name, my number, *Dateline*—I put it together."

"What's the number?" she asked.

He gave it to her.

"Is Echo there?"

"She's in the shower," he said.

"And you're not with her?"

"I have an interview at one of the gaming companies."

Silence.

"You know that saying 'What happens in Vegas stays in Vegas'?" Jordan asked. She didn't answer. He knew that she knew it. "Well, what happened in Tucson doesn't need to stay in Tucson," he ventured.

She understood, but she wasn't ready to go there yet. "I had that CVS test yesterday," she said instead.

"I know," he said. "But first can we talk about—"

"Isn't Echo done in the shower yet?" she asked.

"Would you stop it?"

Weren't moments like the one in Tucson supposed to happen and then pass, become anecdotal memories? One day, when they were both married to other people, they'd laugh about it. Someone would mention Tucson and they'd exchange glances, a shared memory. Sasha would probably roll her eyes and Jordan would wink.

Call waiting sounded, and Sasha pulled away from the phone to look at the incoming number. It was her parents. "Oh! My parents are on the other line."

"Fine," he said.

"I'll call you back."

"Whatever."

She hung up with Jordan, but she didn't answer her parents' call. She'd avoided speaking to them for weeks now, and withholding the information about her pregnancy was killing her. She knew her parents would be there for support, confused but available. But she wanted to be able to present them with a beginning, a middle, and an end, and she couldn't do that just yet. She'd call them once this was all through. She'd call and say, "Mom, Dad, boy, do I have a story for you."

As an only child, Sasha had always been unusually comfortable around adults. She had friends but often found herself conversing with their parents at birthday parties and on school trips. She watched the kids her age at play and wondered how they found pleasure among themselves. It all seemed so silly to her—kicking a ball around, slapping hands, singing songs—even at the age of six. It wasn't until she entered the scholarly field of childhood education that she learned more about the behavior of only children—the tremendous bond between them and their parents, their feelings of connectedness within the family. They often re-created sibling relationships with a best friend, usually one from childhood, which was true of her and Erika. Only children often grew up to be ambitious, successful adults.

Kids often called attention to the fact that she had a friendly relationship with her parents. Some were in awe of it, others disgusted. She could still remember sitting at the kitchen table with her parents and Erika, who had flown in for their friend Gabe Rosenfeld's bar mitzvah. Sasha re-created every scene of the lavish evening, including the one where he pulled her into the bathroom and French-kissed her. Erika kicked her under the table and later chastised her: "You don't have to tell them *everything*!" But she always had. She didn't understand why it was wrong.

But thirteen had been a turning point for Sasha, as, she now realized, it was for most girls. She'd replaced her parents with her friends and a striped purple diary.

twenty

Her senior year of college, lonely from her breakup with Matt Miller, Sasha had buried herself in work. It was a Thursday in October when she walked into her shared apartment and found a guy asleep in her bed. Her roommate was home, so she thought nothing of it. Upon closer inspection, she saw that the lump in her bed had a stubbly blond beard, ratty shirt, and was sleeping so deeply, so vulnerably, that she had felt a surge of love for him, this stranger. She brought her graduate-school applications into the living room. It was late October and most of them were due in December, so on top of her regular workload she was saddled with the stress of personal essays and letters of recommendation.

When she returned to her room to grab another CD, the blob's eyes were open. They were warm and smiley. "Are you Sasha?" he asked. She nodded. "Your bed smells nice."

"You look really peaceful sleeping on it," she said, digging for the CD. "Who are you?"

He was Chad, Billy Lambert's friend from high school. He'd just come back from three months in Indonesia and had a few days in New York before heading back home to Seattle. He'd tried college for a while but didn't want to waste his youth in the classroom, as he put it. He was going to travel the world and then perhaps return to school. Basically, he was the opposite of Sasha.

"And you're in my bed because . . ."

Chad laughed, a little embarrassed. "Billy offered it."

Billy lived across the street and had an extra set of keys, in case of emergency. This wasn't the emergency she'd had in mind. He'd sent Chad over to Sasha's place while he hosted a study group in his own apartment. He intended to pick Chad up when it was over. Sasha found her CD, Stevie Wonder, and sat on the edge of the bed. "I feel like Little Red Riding Hood," she said.

"And I'm the wolf?" Chad asked. She smiled. "Not a wolf," he said. "Just a big pussycat." He scooted over and tapped the empty spot next to him. Sasha complied. Billy was late as usual, so they lay next to each other and talked for the next hour. Suddenly her applications could wait. Chad knew all about Billy's friend Sasha, but he was all new to her. She didn't mean to make him feel bad when she said, "Billy's one of my best friends and I've never even heard of you."

"Maybe it's because I've been away."

"For four years?"

The next half hour was all Indonesia: Bali, Lombok, Sumatra, Borneo. The names as exciting and foreign as Chad himself. The world beckoned while Sasha took midterms, interned at an elementary school, and scraped together rent for a minuscule apartment. Why hadn't she decided to explore the world like Chad, who was now on his side, stretching?

"Fourteen hours in a middle seat," he said, referring to his flight. They'd been side by side for more than an hour when her roommate walked in to ask something. As soon as she saw them, she ran out. "Sorry," she called from the hallway. Sasha was embarrassed, both by her roommate's assumption and by her own need to clarify. But by the time Billy wandered in, another hour later, they really were kissing. That didn't stop him from entering.

"I see you two have met," he said. He joined them on the bed, because he was like that.

It was Sasha who pulled away. "I love when you bring strange men into my bed," she said.

"I can tell," Billy said.

That night the three of them made their way to a Japanese karaoke bar, where they ate mediocre sushi, drank Asahis, and took turns singing duets. As they were leaving, drunk and hoarse, Jordan entered with a group of friends. He waved. Sasha ran up and uncharacteristically high-fived him.

"You're drunk," he said.

"I'm drunk," she sang. He wanted to chat, but she wanted Chad, so she kept on walking. They were on Avenue C, then B, then A, and the whole way home Sasha was concocting a plan to get Chad back to her place alone. They reached Billy's apartment first, and she was surprised when he announced that he'd see them tomorrow. It was easier than she'd imagined.

It was one-thirty in the morning when she closed the bathroom door and inserted, for the first time, the sponge, which she'd gotten at the student-health services last month. She hadn't intended to use it this soon. Her women's studies class last semester, coupled with her breakup with Matt, had encouraged her to stop taking the Pill. Who needed all those hormones rushing through her body? She unwrapped the white concave sponge. It looked like a change purse she'd had as a kid. She closed her eyes as she navigated it up inside. It wasn't an easy fit. Her frustration grew. Why hadn't she practiced beforehand? What would Chad think she was doing in here? "I'll be right out," she called. It was another ten minutes before she was certain it was secure. She flushed the toilet out of habit and hoped he didn't think she'd been on it for that long.

She emerged in a waffled cream-colored robe that her parents had given her last Christmas. Chad was comfortably naked on her bed. It was two, then three, then four in the morning, and they were still sliding around under the covers, over the covers, on the floor. Sasha wanted to feel wild with abandon. Outside her window, the leaves were turning. The chill in the room was just enough to cool her body. At five, when the air was still and the sounds outside were faint, they fell asleep, naked and exhausted—the traveler and the scholar wrapped together.

He postponed his flight to Seattle and stayed in her room, in her bed, for two more days. She went to her classes on Monday but took Tuesday off. Sasha and Chad walked around SoHo, holding hands, buying sunglasses, eating cheese sandwiches. On Wednesday, he left. He kissed her hard on the lips and thanked her with a polite formality usually reserved for distant relatives.

"Do you think you'll come back to New York anytime soon?" Sasha asked as she stood in her doorway.

"No," he said. "Next stop is Mexico."

"Well, I'm sure I'll hear about you from Billy, or if you want to write or anything."

"I'll think of you when I hear 'Islands in the Stream.' "

Great, she thought. How often will that be? And she never found out, because she never heard from Chad again.

~ ~ ~

It was almost ten at night. Sasha was reading when Jordan called. "I think I found Chad," he said. "Turn on the TV."

"Which channel?"

"Fox."

It was a glossy teenage soap opera, one she'd read about but had never seen.

"If it's him, he just stole his mother's car and crashed it into a tree," Jordan said.

"You think he's an actor?"

"Just wait, they'll cut back to him in a sec."

Now a pretty girl was flirting with her math teacher. There were equations on the chalkboard in the background, the girl inching closer and closer. The scene shifted to a banged-up BMW and a motionless guy on a stretcher.

"Is he dead?" Sasha asked.

"I doubt it," Jordan said.

The camera zoomed in on his face. His eyes were nervous, and he was trying to speak. The technician, an equally pretty face, was shushing him. Sasha squatted in front of the TV and cocked her head to the side. Blood trickled down his cheek. If it wasn't Chad from six years ago, it was his twin.

"He's an actor?" Sasha asked again.

"If you can call it acting," Jordan said.

"It's him. It's got to be him," Sasha said. So much for traveling the world.

They stayed on the phone for the duration of the show, not really talking but commenting on the plot points. It finally ended, the potential Chad character in the hospital and the math teacher walking out of his classroom with traces of chalk on his sweater. The show bled right into the ten o'clock news, its credits relegated to the corner of the screen in a tiny, unreadable font.

Sasha ran to her computer and typed in the name of the show. Hundreds of links appeared. She clicked on a cast list and found "Chad Owen as Drew Mackenzie." "His name's Chad, but I don't remember Owen being his last name."

"Hello, Ms. Naive," Jordan said. "Isn't this the city of fake names?"

"And fake ages," Sasha said. "He's my age and he's playing someone in high school?"

"No," Jordan explained. "He's the main girl's brother. He's in community college."

Sasha combed her memory for his last name. She used her mom's technique, a cursory trip down the alphabet. She didn't have to go far. "Ashland!" she said.

"Maybe Owen is his middle name."

"Or maybe it's just not him," Sasha said, knowing that it probably was.

~ ~ ~

It took only a call to her agent the next day to track down Chad. It was Wednesday, her last day off from work. She often forgot that she had an agent. When her show sold over a year ago, a flurry of them had approached her and delivered their spiel. They promised acting gigs, overall deals, and, funniest of all, directing opportunities. None of it appealed to her, but she played along, settling on the agency with the most architecturally stunning building.

Her agent, Dave Devlin, was just out of college—young

and hungry was how he'd described himself. She assumed these were positive attributes. He'd drawn up a contract, had the appropriate parties sign it, and sent her an over-the-top bouquet when the show debuted. She'd never had much reason to call him until now.

"He's over at CAA," Dave told her. "You want to be set up?"

"No," Sasha said. "He's an old friend. I just want to get back in touch."

"You know him? We should find a project for the two of you."

"How about parenthood?" she wanted to say.

"I haven't seen your show yet," he went on, "but keep up the good work. I'm adding all the awards to your résumé."

She had a résumé?

She called Chad's agent at CAA, where an assistant freely gave her his cell-phone number. She called it immediately and left a message: "Hi, Chad. This is Sasha Salter, Billy Lambert's friend. From college. We met years ago. Call me if you can. I'd like to talk to you about something." She left her number and wondered if she'd ever hear back.

She did, in less than half an hour. "Hey, hon, it's Chad."

At first she thought it was Jordan, putting her on. "Hon?"

"What's up, sweetie? How've you been?"

"This is Chad?" she asked.

"Yeah. How's it going?"

Why was he acting as if this was normal? She hadn't seen him in six years. "It's good. I'm good. Everything's good."

"Sweetie, I've got five minutes before I have to get back to the set. You just calling to say hi?"

"Yeah, that and a few other things. There's actually something—"

"Come visit me," he said. "I'm on the Warner Brothers lot. I'll leave you a drive-on."

"Today?" she asked.

"Today," he said, and hung up.

~ ~ ~

Sasha found a spot on the lot and walked toward the soundstage the guard had pointed out. She didn't want to be there on someone else's set; she wanted to be back on her own set, with her own coworkers. In the distance, she spotted a gaggle of kids playing Hacky Sack and laughing uproariously. She thought she recognized one of the girls from a recent cover of a fashion magazine. She could tell, because the girl was all skin and bones. As she approached, it became clear that Chad was among them. He looked the same, only less gaunt and more toned. He was clean-shaven and wore a hideous pair of gold-rimmed sunglasses. He kneed the Sack and then squatted down and let it bounce off his head. Everyone laughed. That's when he spotted Sasha. He immediately left the game and ran over to her.

"Is it you?" he called as he ran.

"It's me," she said, forcing a smile.

She thought he was going to take a flying leap into her arms, but he stopped short and just looked her over. "How you doing, sweetie?"

"I'm good."

"Come meet the posse," he said, taking her by the wrist and leading her over to the circle.

She wasn't in a particularly social mood, and although she knew these were stars of a hot new show and that she should retain their names for future storytelling, she stood there, disconnected, nodding as he introduced them.

". . . Callie, Steve-O, Ms. Rachel, Tom, Brett, and Petra."

Petra was the skinny one. Up close, she was angular and hard to look at. Next, he led her to his trailer a few feet away. It smelled of pot and leather. "Can I grab you a beer?" he asked. Not only was she pregnant; it was eleven in the morning. She hoped he didn't grab one himself. The smell would surely put her over the edge.

"Do you still talk to Billy?" she asked.

"Nah. Last time I saw him was about the last time I saw you," he said, pulling a bottled water from the mini-fridge.

"I thought you guys were great friends," she said.

He shrugged. "Things change."

Chad gulped down the water, darting his tongue in and out of the bottle. Sasha vaguely remembered when he did that to her. He took off his sunglasses. His eyes had an intensity she hadn't remembered.

"Well, I have kind of a crazy story," she started.

"Yeah? Let's hear it."

"There's this condition, it's really rare. *Lazicum spermatozoa.*" Chad's gaze intensified. "It's a combination of a very hospitable environment coupled with a tenacious sperm, for whatever reason." She knew she wasn't explaining it well and at this point Chad tuned out. He picked at the label on the water. He seemed bored. "It's like the planets aligned, but in all the wrong ways," she said. "Basically, I'm pregnant. And there's a remote possibility it's yours."

Chad capped his water bottle, looked up at her, and threw it across the room. He stood up as it hit the wall and then dropped to the floor. "Fuck you," he said. "You can't do this to me." Sasha's heart leaped into her throat. What was he going to do next?

"I'm working with a doctor," she said quickly, trying to explain before he threw something else. "This is his specialty. I'm supposed to collect blood and tissue samples from anyone I've slept with. For DNA. I know it seems weird—"

"Do you think I'm an asshole? You think I'm just a dumb actor? I took biology! This isn't how it works. You think I'm an idiot?"

She did think he was an asshole. She did think he was an idiot. But not for those reasons.

"What do you want?" he asked, crossing the room to pick up the bottle and tossing it into the trash by the door. He missed. "How much do you need? This is what my career has turned into? Paying hush money?"

"I don't want money," Sasha clarified, raising her voice. "I just need blood and tissue samples."

"Fuck you and the horse you rode in on," he sneered. She wondered if that was a line from his show, minus the expletive.

"Chad, I don't care that you're an actor. I work in television, too. I don't need your money. This is a highly unusual situation."

"My lawyer warned me this was gonna happen," he said, pacing now.

Sasha shook her head, trying to figure out a way to get through to him.

"Now what?" he asked. "You're taking the story to the *Enquirer*? *Access Hollywood*? *Celebrity Justice*? Fine. Go. Do it."

Aside from the *Enquirer*, she didn't know what he was talking about. She wondered if she should have Dr. Rusmeuth contact him. "Chad, like I said, this is highly unusual. I know we were together six years ago."

"We weren't *together,* I *fucked* you."

She hated this guy. "Maybe you picked up some bug traveling around in Thailand. Maybe it affected your sperm. How do you know it's not possible?"

"Don't play me" was all he said. What did it even mean to *play* someone? Was it possible he'd *played* her six years ago?

Sasha stood up. She was suffocating from the energy in the room. She had to get out of the trailer, off the Warner Brothers lot.

"Where are you going?" he asked.

"To work," she said. "I work. I host a TV show. I've won an Emmy. I do something that matters," she said, heading to the door.

"I'm dating Petra," he said, trying to trump her.

She made it to the door and opened it. Sunlight brightened the dark interior. Sasha blinked a few times. Chad reached over and closed the door. The light vanished and she couldn't see a thing.

"Whatever's going on," he said, "I don't want you back here. I'll get a restraining order."

Sasha waited for her eyesight to return to normal. When it did, she dug in her purse and extracted Dr. Rusmeuth's card. Her hand was shaking as she passed it to him. "Please," she said. He took the card and looked it over before tossing it aside. Then she saw the empty bottle of water and picked it up. "Oh, yeah," she said. "I also recycle." With that she opened the door and walked out of the trailer, past the cast playing Hacky Sack and back to the safety of her car. She drove off the lot and over to Dr. Rusmeuth's office, hoping that he could at least swab the bottle for Chad's DNA.

Sasha called from the car. MaryAnne picked up. "Doctor's office," she said.

"I have another sample," Sasha said, adrenaline pumping. "I have it in my car. What do I do with it?" Sasha waited a second before she clarified. "This is Sasha Salter."

"You've drawn blood from someone?" MaryAnne said, confused.

"No! It's more like a buccal swab," she said. "I've got a water bottle with someone's saliva on it."

"Dr. Rusmeuth's not here right now," MaryAnne said. "But let me give you the telephone number of the lab we use." Sasha heard papers rustling in the background.

"Just give me the address," Sasha said. "I'm in the car, I'll go there now." She looked at the water bottle in the passenger seat.

"Oooh, I don't know if I—"

"MaryAnne?" Sasha said. "Give. Me. The. Address." When she got it, she sped into Santa Monica and hand-delivered the final sample. She filled out some paperwork, writing "DNA 827" and below it in bold capital letters: **EXPEDITE**.

~ ~ ~

On Thursday, Sasha was excited to finally get back to work, but after an hour it was clear that something was wrong: everyone was handling her with kid gloves. Pam spoke slowly and loudly, as though Sasha had trouble understanding English. Fritz kept his distance when normally he was a touchy, effusive person. It crossed her mind that perhaps she was being paranoid, but when Sarah suggested that they break early for lunch because Sasha looked pale, she knew something was up.

She ran to her dressing room and looked in the mirror. She didn't look pale. She squinted her eyes to find the pallor, but it never emerged. She looked plump, zaftig. So far, the biggest pregnancy-related craving she had was for normalcy. Unfortunately, she couldn't pick that up at the corner store. Sasha used the early lunch break wisely. She donned her English accent and called the *Dateline* producer.

"This is Gail," the producer said.

"This is Lisa," Sasha said. "I'm cawling about the segment you're airing this weekend. It could be too late, but there's a doctor I know whom you might want to speak with. Dr. Rusmeuth."

"Ira Rusmeuth," Gail said. "That's the doctor we're featuring. Who is this?"

"From Los Angeles?" Sasha asked in her own voice.

"Yes, that's him. Who may I ask is—"

Sasha threw the cell phone across the room. Her fears were realized. Her doctor, her case. The animated silhouette of the person, Sasha. She remembered how cautious he was the day she walked into his office a month ago. And then how caution had given way to excitement, excitement to exuberance. If only he'd been able to contain it. The one thing Sasha could do now, the only power she had, was to leave him.

twenty-one

Sasha entered the building, a force to be reckoned with. She bypassed the elevator and instead climbed the stairs to Dr. Rusmeuth's office. She entered the waiting room and found, to her surprise, a man sitting in one of the chairs. In all the times she'd been to Rusmeuth's office, she'd never seen another patient. As soon as he saw her, he hid behind an issue of *Golf Digest*.

MaryAnne was behind the front desk. She slid open the window. "Sasha! Were we expecting you?" she asked, an eyebrow arched.

"I need to see Dr. Rusmeuth immediately," she said. She would not take no for an answer. She tricked a mantra around in her brain: *She can't say no, she can't say no.*

"He's with a patient right now, and he's got another one waiting." She pointed to the man behind the magazine.

She can't say no.

Sasha stuck her head past the partition so that she was face-to-face with MaryAnne. She spoke in a cold, calculated manner—the tone she'd taken with Melanie the week before. "I need to see Rusmeuth immediately." She dropped the "doctor." He didn't deserve the respect. MaryAnne looked scared. She rolled her chair back, stood up, and disappeared into the office. She returned a minute later with Sasha's chart and motioned for her to come through. "Follow me," she said, leading her into a room.

"I am disgusted by this office," Sasha said in a loud voice. MaryAnne dropped the folder into the slot and quickly walked back to her post.

By now, Sasha was fuming. Just because Dr. Rusmeuth had named the condition didn't mean it belonged to him, didn't mean he could go on *Dateline* and tell her story. This was *her* problem. How could he take credit for this trick of nature? She paced the room for a few moments and then sat on the examination table, the tissue paper crinkling under her weight. The longer he didn't arrive, the angrier she became. She wondered if she'd feel the same way if he'd called to warn her that he was going on television to reveal the anomaly. Could he possibly still think she'd be interested in letting him adopt her child? Did he think she *owed* him this child?

Then he knocked on the door and entered. He looked everywhere but into her eyes. She followed his erratic gaze, determined not to let him get away with it. "I won't be needing your services anymore," she finally blurted out.

Rusmeuth thumbed through her chart. She reached over and plucked it out of his hands, just like that. She wondered if he'd try to grab it back. She tightened her grip. He looked naked standing there without the chart. His hands had nothing to do, so he crossed them over his chest. "Sasha."

She realized there was a remote possibility that he didn't

know why she was so angry. She looked at him while contemplating her next move. Before she said anything, he spoke. "I think I know why you're concerned, but this is just a bad coincidence."

"Oh, so you know why I'm here?" she said, clinging to her chart.

"*Dateline* came to me, I didn't seek them out."

Something didn't sit right. In his twenty years of research, why was this the first time the media had got wind of his work? And of all the doctors, why him? Worse, why when she was his patient? "Why do I have the feeling you need me more than I need you?" she asked.

"You don't have anything to worry about," he said dismissively. "I didn't speak to them in any detail. I certainly didn't mention your name. Our interview was mainly about men's fertility issues, Sasha. You have to believe me."

"I don't have to do anything," she said.

The doctor brought his fist to his mouth. He looked as if he was strategizing his next move.

"Imagine my surprise when I saw the commercial for *Dateline,*" she said.

Rusmeuth shook his head. "I can't imagine," he said. "Really."

"A letter, a phone call, an e-mail might have been appropriate."

"Sasha, you have to understand, I've hypothesized about *Lazicum spermatozoa* for over a decade."

"Yes, but *you* have to understand that it's not just some abstract concept anymore! There's now a person attached. *I'm* attached. And my entire life, my entire career is at stake. I'm afraid you're not a very good people person, Mr. Rusmeuth."

"Dr. Rusmeuth."

"Well, as I said, I won't be needing your services anymore, *Dr.* Rusmeuth." She started to slide off the table.

"But you haven't even seen the episode yet. Don't you think you should wait to see the episode before you walk away?"

Why was he trying to tell her what to do?

"This is all very upsetting, and exciting, and—" Dr. Rusmeuth started.

"I don't find this very exciting," Sasha interrupted. "See, I find this to be a bit of a nightmare, actually, an inconvenience, a major disturbance."

Rusmeuth let out a breath. He refocused. Just as he was about to speak, Sasha's cell phone sounded that unusual ring. "Shit." She grabbed the phone from her bag. It was a text message, simple and alarming: "Erika had baby." Sasha hopped off the table and pushed past Rusmeuth, who was standing in the doorway.

She got into her car and made her way across town, and as she pulled into the outpatient parking lot she reflected that she'd gone from the doctor's office to the hospital all before noon.

~ ~ ~

Erika was winded by the time Sasha entered the room. She looked as if she'd just finished competing in a triathlon and was sucking on ice chips to cool down. Jeff held the baby, a boy, still nameless. His eyes were open, but he didn't seem awake.

"Hi, Aunt Sasha," Jeff said.

"Hi, everyone." Sasha didn't know whom to approach first—her best friend in the bed or the new one, swathed in a yellow blanket.

Erika wiggled her fingers in a gesture of hello. "Go meet your nephew," she said in a voice watery from exhaustion.

Jeff offered the baby to Sasha, but she didn't feel comfortable taking him standing up. She grabbed the chair next to Erika's bed and dragged it into the middle of the room. Then she extended her arms as Jeff placed the baby in them.

He wriggled at first and made a pre-cry face, but soon he settled into a comfortable stare. Sasha could feel his warmth through the blanket; it emanated, steady and unapologetic, onto her lap. His head rested in the crook of her inner elbow, his tufts of hair tickling her. He was solid, firm, alive.

"My boobs are killing me," Erika said. "When do I have to feed him?"

"In about half an hour," Jeff said, sitting on the edge of the bed. "Isn't he perfect?" he asked Sasha.

She wanted to say yes, but she couldn't find her voice.

"He'll be more perfect when he has a name," Erika said.

"Baby steps," Jeff said, and both of them laughed.

Sasha concentrated on his nose, which sat pink and perfect in the middle of his face. She put a finger under it to feel his warm, shallow breath. She was trembling suddenly. She didn't know when it had started.

"I can't do this," Sasha finally said. She lifted the baby and Jeff hopped off the bed, scooping him out of her arms. "I love you guys," she said as she headed to the door.

"We love you, too," Erika said.

Sasha walked down the hospital halls at a fast clip. Erika hadn't even questioned why Sasha left. At that moment, Sasha realized why she loved Erika so much. Never a question, never a judgment. Sasha drove home in her Saab, the smell of the baby lingering on her skin.

It's only a shrimp, she kept telling herself, as her decision crystallized on the twelve-minute drive home. It doesn't yet have a nose, eyelashes, nails. She couldn't care for a child yet, alone, with painful boobs. "When do I have to feed him?" she'd ask, but of whom? She couldn't be a mom now. There was something about Erika's baby's nose, pink and needy in the middle of his face. Something clicked. She was never attached, only disconnected. The shrimp inside was sexless, personalityless, a growth. It had to be removed.

She called Fritz at work. "Tell Pam I'm taking the rest of the day off," she said. "Fax me the script at home. Don't worry, I'll be ready for tomorrow."

"Sasha, are you o—"

"Just . . . please?" she said before hanging up.

She arrived at home and jumped out of her car to call Dr. Banks. There was a broken signal on her phone, indicating messages, but she didn't have time to check them. It was probably her parents calling again, worried.

Dr. Banks took her call immediately. "Sasha! Did you get my messages?"

"I just walked in."

"The lab called. We have the results."

A wave of nausea crested in the middle of Sasha's belly and slowly moved upward. "I'm actually calling because I've made a decision," she said quickly. "I need to terminate."

Silence replaced their voices. Dr. Banks finally broke it. "I respect your decision," she said. "But don't you want to know about the sperm?"

Sasha had always wondered how, in movies, books, and television shows, a character could receive a letter and opt not to read it. She would burn it, throw it away, place it in a drawer with a million other unopened letters. Sasha never believed those moments. They never rang true. If she were in a movie right now, her character would probably slam down the phone and drag herself to the abortion clinic, leaving the answer dangling midair like a bad smell. She couldn't. This was real life, and curiosity was a natural part of it. She sighed. "I do," she said.

"Can you come in now?" Dr. Banks asked.

"I can," Sasha said.

"Listen," Dr. Banks said. "Are you seeing the therapist I referred you to?"

"No, but I have someone else I'd like to bring."

~ ~ ~

"I'm Klara Banks," the doctor said to Jordan as she shepherded them into her large office. It was both hilarious and horrifying to see Jordan there, surrounded by pictures of female anatomy. It felt like such a sacred space. Dr. Banks closed the door. To Sasha, it felt like Dr. Banks was moving through molasses. When she returned to her desk, she ran a finger down a piece of paper. "One point four six three," she said under her breath.

"What?" Sasha asked.

Dr. Banks took that same finger and moved it to another paper on her desk. "One point four six three," she said again. She looked up. "The DNA belongs to Chad. I don't see a last name here."

"Ashland," Jordan said.

Sasha reached out and took Jordan's hand.

"Are you okay?" he asked.

"No," she said. "Are you sure?" she asked Dr. Banks. "Are you positive?"

"It's a match," Dr. Banks said.

Sasha squeezed Jordan's hand. Her heart was pounding. She thought about the scene from Chad's TV show—Chad on a stretcher after crashing his mother's car. He lay speechless, unable to move, but his eyes were full of expression: fear, horror, pain. She imagined he'd look the same way when she told him he was the owner of the lazy sperm, the father of her child. How could she possibly tell him this news?

"Now what?" Sasha asked, her voice hollow. She felt like she was about to cry, but suddenly the lump in her throat dissolved. Her frown flipped into a smile and she started laughing. Dr. Banks and Jordan looked at her. Their expressions only made her laugh harder. And when they turned to each other she was on the edge of hysterics.

Dr. Banks took off her glasses and smiled at Sasha. Jordan did the same. His smile was so safe and familiar and warm. He was smiling with her, not at her. She pointed to his mouth, and when he said "What?" she burst into a new wave of laughter. Dr. Banks leaned back in her chair.

"I'm sorry," Sasha finally said. She was running out of breath, and it sounded like "I'm sa," which only set her off again. A few seconds later, she was crying. Hard. She wasn't sure when the transition took place. Her face was wet and her vision was blurred. Dr. Banks sat forward and handed her some tissues. Jordan took them and passed them to her.

This had happened only once before, this strange laugh/cry phenomenon. She had been in a yoga class with Erika when she first moved to L.A., stressed and overwhelmed. She was amazed that she could get into many poses without a fuss. The teacher was even surprised she'd never taken a class before. But when she got into Bow Pose, lying on her stomach, her arms grasping her ankles, she'd started laughing. She didn't come out of the pose even when her laughter turned to crying. Erika was in the Bow next to her, trying not to look, but when the tears started she summoned the teacher, who eased Sasha out of the pose and told her she could stay in Child's Pose for the rest of the class. It was the first and last yoga class she'd ever taken.

"This is a lot to handle," Dr. Banks said gently. "It's okay."

It felt like another half hour, but it was probably only a few minutes before the swells settled and Sasha could once again be present, focused. At some point, Jordan had moved his chair closer to hers and had his arm around her back. When she was calm, he removed it.

"Chad's an actor," she said. "I was never in a relationship with him; it was more of a fling, about six years ago."

Dr. Banks raised her eyebrows. "Six years ago," she said. "Imagine that." She looked back at her paperwork. "You'd been using the sponge at that time?" Sasha nodded. Dr. Banks wrote something down. "According to Dr. Rusmeuth, it's possible that a tiny, even minuscule, piece of the sponge broke off and was able to host Mr. Ashland's sperm."

"For six years?" Jordan said. "Jesus."

"I can't deal with Dr. Rusmeuth," Sasha said. She looked to Jordan for support.

"He really violated her trust," he said.

"And it was completely inappropriate for him to even suggest that he wanted to adopt this baby," Sasha said.

"What do you want to do, Sasha?" Dr. Banks asked.

Sasha didn't answer. She couldn't.

Dr. Banks shook her head. "Ira," she said. She started to say something else, but then she stopped.

"What?" Sasha asked.

Dr. Banks considered. "Ira and I . . ." She corrected herself. "Dr. Rusmeuth and I met in medical school," she said. "He was always an unconventional thinker." She laughed at a memory but didn't share it. "He was asked to leave Stanford because he was, quote, too imaginative."

"He didn't go to medical school?" Jordan asked.

"He did. He transferred," Dr. Banks said.

"He was too imaginative?" Sasha found it hard to believe.

"Since the day I met him, he's always thought out of the box," Dr. Banks confirmed.

"No pun intended," Jordan said. Sasha shot him a look.

Dr. Banks looked at her imploringly. "I understand why you don't want to see him," she said. "I really do. But it's hard to overlook the enormous significance of the fact that his cockamamy theory turned out to be true."

"His theory, my life," Sasha said.

"Of course," Dr. Banks said.

"And I need to get on with my life," Sasha said. "This isn't funny anymore." The entire scenario still seemed like a cosmic joke.

"Was it ever?" Jordan asked.

~ ~ ~

At home later that night, Sasha opened the door to find Fritz. She was completely surprised. She threw her arms around him for a big hug. When she pulled back, she noticed that he looked gaunt and sullen.

"Come in," she said. "What's wrong?"

"Nothing, I just miss you," he said. "We all miss you."

They sat at the kitchen table. Sasha made tea.

"I miss you, too," Sasha said. "I got your fax. Don't worry about tomorrow. I'll be fine."

"I am worried," he said.

"About tomorrow?"

"About you."

Here it was again: another case of the lies. He'd express his concerns, and she'd have to lie them away. She inhaled and waited for him to speak. He didn't. Fritz was looking into his tea mug, his glasses fogged by the heat of the water. She exhaled.

"Mel dumped me," he finally said.

In the year and a half that she'd worked with Fritz, Sasha had always wondered if he was gay. She finally had her answer. "He did?" she said.

"He? Sasha, *Melanie*—the one writing the article about you."

"That fucking bitch," Sasha said, surprising herself.

"I was in love with that *fucking bitch,*" he said. "Just so you know."

She covered her mouth. "I'm sorry," she said, softening. "How long were you together?"

"Three weeks today," he said. "It might not sound like a lot to you, but we were doing good. I was getting used to her being around." And then, "Are you dying?" He gazed up at her over the mug and then quickly looked down. "That just came out. I didn't mean to be so blunt."

Sasha swirled her tea bag and watched as green puffs of mint leaked into the water. "I'm so not dying," she said. The truth escaped in her next breath. "I'm the exact opposite of dying."

She wondered what everyone else at work thought. Fritz had always been her ear to the ground. He looked confused. He brought his mug back down to the table. "I'm pregnant," she said. The weight of the words floated up, up and away.

"Oh, my God," he said. He seemed sincerely shocked. "How far along?" A smile crossed his face and he looked at her belly. "This is so cool!"

"You're the first person from work I've told. I'm completely freaked out. There goes the show, right?" she asked. "G-rated Sasha Salter gets knocked up and ruins her reputation in the kids' world."

"Yeah, if this was 1950," Fritz said. "Maybe you could do another show," he suggested, "*Please Pass the Condoms.*" They both laughed. Fritz stood up and hugged Sasha. "Congratulations. I had you dying."

"It was completely unexpected," Sasha said. "There's so much to it, I can't even begin to tell you."

"It's okay," he said. "Whenever you're ready. Or not."

"I'm probably not keeping it," she said, searching hard in his eyes for his thoughts.

Fritz lifted his hands. "No judgment," he said.

She reminded him one more time. "You are the *only* one who knows about this."

"And you're the only one who knows how heartbroken I am," he said. He took a thoughtful pause. "Melanie and I had the best sex I've ever had in my life."

Sasha didn't mean to, but she shook her head.

"And now she's off to New York."

"She's moving there?" Sasha asked.

"She got a job at *Dateline,*" Fritz said.

Sasha choked on the sip of tea.

"She picked some fucking news show over me," he said. "What was wrong with her fucking magazine job?"

"*Dateline,*" Sasha said.

"You know that show, right?" Fritz said.

"I do."

"I didn't even know she was looking for work," he said. "It never came up. Don't you think that's weird?"

It *was* Melanie, hot on her trail from the beginning. The little bitch should have been a detective, a private dick. And now Sasha's situation had landed the twit a plum job at *Dateline*. Of course she couldn't say any of this to brokenhearted Fritz. "Sounds like she's a career girl," she said instead.

"Oh!" Fritz said, suddenly remembering something. He pulled a manila envelope out of his bag. "She wanted me to give you this."

Sasha wondered what it contained. She thanked Fritz, put the envelope on the table, and escorted him to the door. "I'll see you tomorrow," she told him. "Promise you won't worry about me. I'm a professional."

"Don't I know it," he said before leaving.

~ ~ ~

Sasha ripped open the envelope. Inside was a copyedited version of the article Melanie had written.

WHY YOUR KIDS LOVE SASHA SALTER

by Melanie Fitzpatrick

She makes them laugh, and when they laugh fifteen facial muscles contract, their blood pressure lowers, their diaphragm, abdominal, respiratory, facial, leg, and back muscles get a workout. Laughter brings balance to all the components of the immune system, and Sasha Salter (27) makes sure it happens once a week. Sasha knows what makes your kids tick, from physical humor to word play to silly songs. Kids love her for it. If they're lucky enough to see a live taping, they line up after the show to get her autograph and she complies. The line would move quicker if she would abbreviate her name for the signature, "but SS just doesn't feel right." Now that's funny.

Sasha Salter runs a lot, but not in an exercise way. She runs to meetings, to rehearsals, to photo shoots, to appointments. Sometimes she's a blur, like the Road Runner escaping from a prank. Other times, like onstage rehearsing a sketch, she's present and focused. Entertaining your kids is serious business. What makes *her* laugh? "Everything," Salter says. "Life." For now, she's got a lot to chuckle about. Her show, *Please Pass the Salter*, which derived from her master's degree thesis on Developmental Psychology, has won numerous awards and is headed for more. "No man, or woman, is an island," she says. "I'm just a link in a chain of events that happened to spawn a terrific show." Sasha Salter is modest, and modesty is a good quality for your kids to observe. So next Saturday morning when you plop them in front of *Please Pass the Salter*, don't worry, Sasha works hard to make sure it's good for them, and that is why we vote her number eleven in *20 Under 30—Ones to Watch.*

Sasha put aside the article. *Number eleven?*

An envelope slipped out and onto the floor. Sasha retrieved it. On flowery stationery was scrawled:

Hi, Sasha,

Here it is—hope you approve of the article! Sorry we never got to say goodbye. As you may have heard, I'm moving to New York to take a job at Dateline*—and ultimately I have you to thank. I could tell something was wrong the first time I went to the doctor with you. You seemed stunned. Curiosity got the better of me, and the next day I followed you to Dr.*

Rusmeuth's office and, after you left, tripped into the wild world of Lazicum spermatozoa. *Who knew I'd be so good at investigative reporting? When I pitched the concept to* Dateline, *they hired me on the spot, but I had no idea that Rusmeuth would be so forthcoming in his on-camera interview. I mean he didn't name names, but he divulged your profession and hinted at various other things so that anybody who knew your show would know he was talking about you. When I saw the final cut of the segment, I was stunned. Fortunately, I managed to get the story shelved until we could interview some more professional doctors. So you don't have to worry—on Friday night you'll see a rerun about mattresses. We might air the episode later on down the road, but I promise it won't reveal your name in any way. Please know that I never intended for this to happen! I only wanted to expose the condition, not you. You remind me of the person I want to be, Sasha. Thank you for giving that to me. If I hear you've had a baby, I'll know the outcome of your ordeal. And please don't worry, your secret is safe with me.*

Melanie

twenty-two

Sasha was lying under the covers, fully clothed. Dr. Banks had told her to sleep on her decision, and although she'd started the day ready to say goodbye, she'd ended it with more confusion. She was staring at the closet door, imagining that behind it was a world she could enter, like Narnia, where none of this was possible. A world that had order and reason and meaning. Jordan called and asked what she was doing. She couldn't explain, so she said, "Nothing." He said he'd like to come over, but she said she'd rather be alone. Then he phrased it another way—"I *need* to come over," he said. "I *need* to be with you." She couldn't imagine why coming over would make him feel better, but she thought perhaps it was time she acted as his safety net for once, and so she said yes.

After he arrived, he said he wanted to spend the night. She thought he might end up on the living-room sofa, but he ended up in her bed. It was an hour later, and now they were both lying under the covers, fully clothed.

"Do you remember the gloves from Boston?" he asked after a lengthy period of silence.

"What made you think of that?" she said.

"I don't know."

Sasha was home for Christmas break in their sophomore year of college. Jordan had called one night to say that he was coming to Boston to visit his aunt for a few days. It was still early in their friendship, and Sasha was excited to see him in another setting. She was dating Matt, but he'd left to be with his family in Chicago.

Sasha had picked Jordan up at the train station; he had a backpack and a winter coat. They had four hours to kill before his aunt came to take him to Marblehead. Sasha showed him around. They had lunch on Newbury Street and went to Filene's Basement, which Jordan said he'd heard about but needed to see to believe.

Filene's was frenzied with post-Christmas shoppers. Sasha explained how it worked—how prices got marked down from one day to the next, and if you were a true bargain hunter, with time to spare, you could get great deals. She'd picked up a pair of green leather gloves and tried them on. They looked sleek and snug around her hands. She wiggled her fingers at Jordan, traced his cheek with her finger. She looked at the price. "Forty-two dollars today, thirty-one dollars tomorrow, and twenty-six the next," she said. "Now follow me."

Jordan followed her to a nearby bin of toddler clothes. Sasha dug underneath the heap and placed the green gloves there. "You're kidding," he said.

"In two days I come back, dig through this pile, and voilà! Cheap gloves."

"How do you know you'll remember where you put them? What if someone else finds them?" He seemed genuinely concerned, nervous.

"Trust me, I've been doing this for years."

Later, they walked through the Common and, when the time came, met his aunt in front of the Four Seasons. But two days later, when Sasha stopped by Filene's, she couldn't find the gloves. She tore through the toddler bin, but to no avail. They really were gone.

Sasha and Matt spent the first few days back from Christmas vacation locked in her dorm room. Consumed by the skippy feeling of new love, they clung to each other, overwhelmed by their three-week separation.

When Jordan returned to school a few days later, he came over and handed her a wrapped gift.

"For me? Really?"

Matt was on her bed with his shirt off, and Jordan waved before leaving. "Hey, man!"

Inside were the green gloves.

"Why is he buying you presents?" Matt asked later, peering into the box.

"It's just a joke," she said. She tossed the gift aside and fell back into Matt's arms, but she was consumed by the thought of Jordan returning to the store, digging through the piles of clothes, and extracting the gloves. Her heart swelled at his gesture of kindness, the effort, and ached at the delivery—he certainly hadn't expected to find Matt half-naked in her bed. That night, while they were making love, Sasha looked at the box on the floor, the green gloves peeking over, ten fingers calling to her.

Sasha got out of bed and walked to her closet. Tucked in a bottom drawer were her winter clothes. She immediately found the gloves, slipped them on, and returned to bed. They were worn from wear, a little loose in the palms, but they still kept her warm. Jordan laced his hand around her gloved hand, rubbing his thumb against hers.

"I made my aunt drop me off at Filene's that day. She thought I'd miss my train," he said.

"Did you?"

"I caught the next one."

She covered his thumb with hers, and he did the same back.

"I thought I'd go in there and find them, like you said, but I swear it took me an hour." He took her gloved hand in his. "When I found them, it was like I'd struck gold."

"And seven years later I'm still wearing them."

Sasha and Jordan looked at each other. He tugged at the glove and it came right off. They laughed.

"I'm getting tired," she said. "Do you mind if we go to sleep?" She didn't wait for him to answer. She stood up again and took her pajamas into the bathroom, where she changed. They were flannel and had sheep on them. She got back into bed.

"Too cute," Jordan said.

"They're so old."

"Can I see?" Jordan asked.

Sasha sat up to expose more of the pattern.

"Not that," Jordan said. "Let me see that stomach."

Sasha pulled down the pants a little and hitched up the shirt to expose her belly. Jordan tapped it with his finger. "Hello?" he called.

"Stop," Sasha said. She lay on her back, her stomach still exposed. Jordan leaned on his elbow and switched from tapping to rubbing.

"So what does Echo think you're up to tonight?" she asked. It felt good being touched.

"We're done, Sasha," he said.

"Not because of me," she said.

"All you need to know is that we're done."

"I'm sorry," she said. She leaned in and gave him a kiss on the cheek. She detected the faintest smell of aftershave. She rested there a minute before pulling away.

"Wait," Jordan said. "I have to tell you something." He leaned in, bypassing her own cheek and heading straight for her lips.

We meet again, Sasha thought, but this time it felt right and familiar and sincere. Their noses bumped and their teeth clacked and they laughed, but no one pulled away.

They kissed until she fell asleep.

That's when it happened, deep in the recesses of sleep. She knew she was dreaming, but at the same time she didn't. It was winter, and Sasha and Jordan were slogging through the snow. They were somewhere familiar, maybe Boston Common, but maybe not. Sasha was wearing the green gloves, but her fingers were cold. Her feet moved in slow motion. "I can't get warm," she said, but when she looked up Jordan had disappeared. "He'll be back," she told herself, though she didn't know where he'd gone. She kept walking, shoving her hands into her coat pockets for warmth. It was as though she'd walked ten miles before someone appeared—a woman, perhaps her grandmother. "I'm taking a walk with Jordan," Sasha said. The woman shrugged. "You're not walking with anyone, dear," she said. "You never were."

Sasha woke with a start. Jordan was sleeping comfortably on the other side of the bed. She was so relieved to see him that she rolled over and grabbed him. "You're here!" she said.

He laughed sleepily but didn't say anything.

"I dreamt you were gone. But not just gone. Never here, gone."

"That's weird," he said.

"I don't know what all this means," she said.

"What part?"

"All of it," she said. "Was that my sign or something? Am I keeping this?" She pointed to her belly. "Are we dating now?"

"Your sign?" Jordan said.

"If you were never here, that means you were never born. If you had never been born, you wouldn't be here, literally, next to me."

"Are you still dreaming?" he asked.

"Who knows what this baby could be—in life, for somebody."

Jordan turned around and looked at her. "You're keeping it?"

She sighed. "I can't."

Jordan cleared his throat and sat up in bed. He was still in a sweater and jeans. Everything was rumpled.

"I'm not Erika," she said.

"No one's asking you to be."

"A baby?" she said. "A mother?"

"You're kidding, right?" Jordan said. "You only entertain practically every kid in America on a weekly basis."

"With help," Sasha said.

"With help," Jordan said. "Everyone needs help."

"My head is spinning."

"Just breathe," he said.

She did. Her thoughts became clearer. "I have to call Dr. Banks," Sasha said.

"It's two in the morning."

"She said any time."

"Let the woman sleep," Jordan said.

They were quiet for a few moments.

"Am I having a baby?" Sasha finally asked in a small voice.

"I don't know," Jordan said. "Sounds like we might be."

August

twenty-three

The baby shower was finally here, and after all the debate, Sasha was glad she'd decided in favor of it. Erika's mania had reached a fever pitch last week, with eleventh-hour phone calls about centerpieces and gift registries. Sasha begged her to find giant cutout sperm centerpieces rather than the stork Erika suggested, but eventually they settled on fresh-cut daisies in baby bottles. Erika was unusually pushy about having the event at the Four Seasons hotel, where she'd had hers, but when Pam offered her house in Bel Air, Sasha had gratefully accepted.

Spilling the beans at work had been even more trying, more stressful than telling her parents. Work didn't offer the safety net of unconditional love. Work hadn't given birth to Sasha and raised her. Her parents were, as she'd predicted, confused but supportive, inundating her with the same questions she'd posed long ago to her various doctors. As for work, Sasha had called a meeting with Pam and Sarah and added Fritz for moral support. They filed into her dressing room casual and chatty. Fritz winked as he closed the door behind him. When everyone was comfortably seated, Sasha announced, "In a crazy twist of fate, I find that I'm pregnant." Initially there was silence, but then Fritz, ever the actor, jumped up and hugged her. "Congratulations!" Pam followed, stiff at first but then relaxing into the hug. Only Sarah had the reaction Sasha feared. "How are we going to tape?" she asked from the couch. "I mean once she starts showing." Sasha prayed, Please don't let this end the show. Pam, in her calm manner, suggested that they telephone Lewis Adler, the network executive who'd nixed the idea for a hiatus months earlier. Sasha inwardly cringed at the thought. He made her jumpy, and the current situation would only magnify how she already felt about him. Still, these were the consequences of her situation, and she had to take a deep breath, hold her head up high, and reenter the lion's den.

It wasn't easy. All her fears were realized. When she blurted out her news, she was met with a seemingly infinite silence. She wanted desperately to fill it, but she refrained. She rolled her eyes, tapped her feet, sniffed. "I'm speechless," Adler finally said. His words cut through her, but at least he'd spoken.

"Then you can imagine how I felt when they told me," Sasha said.

He was angry, misogynistic, hostile, argumentative, just like a seasoned network executive. She rode each emotion, telling herself not to take it personally. In her new, cool mindset she was able to answer all his questions, suggest alternative ideas, and ultimately rally to keep the show on the air. He repeatedly threatened to end it. It was the only power he wielded. He certainly didn't have the power of giving birth.

She reasoned with him as though she were a hostage reasoning with her captor. And then finally, gently, she won. The show would stay. Wardrobe could be altered. Just because she'd have a belly didn't mean she'd lose her brain. Or ambition. Or talent.

~ ~ ~

Much to Erika's dismay, the shower was coed. Jordan arrived half an hour early, and he and Sasha stood by a table tossing names around.

"Orson," he said. "Don't you love it?"

"Yeah, if my last name was Welles," she said. "How about Karina?"

"Penelope."

"You're fucking kidding, right?"

Jordan covered her belly with both his hands. "Shh. You don't want Penny coming out of the womb swearing."

"I don't want anyone named Penny coming out of me," she said. "Plus, I'm really feeling boy."

"Homer," he said.

"What's with *The Odyssey*?"

"So Agamemnon's out?"

Sasha checked him with her hip and he stumbled back a few steps. She covered her mouth with her hand and he charged her with a hug. It was Jordan who had ultimately inspired Sasha to keep the baby, and it was the baby who had finally nudged her and Jordan together. Though she was still lukewarm about raising a kid, Jordan's enthusiasm was infectious. Through his eyes, she saw that she could be a capable, nurturing, entertaining parent, and he her coparent. He suggested that they get married, but she'd said one life-altering event at a time, please. That night in bed after the meeting with Dr. Banks, he'd said he wanted clarification. He'd asked what he was to her, and she simply answered, "Everything."

"You're one hot mama," he said now, kissing her.

Erika approached midkiss. "Watch it," she said. "This one gets pregnant in crazy ways."

"Where's Austin?" Jordan asked, referring to her son.

"With my parents."

"But you love being a mom, right?" Sasha asked, half kidding.

"Are you having second thoughts?" Erika said.

"No. Just clarifying."

"I love being a mom," Erika said, and smiled. "For the record, I also love sleeping, but I'm sure I'll catch up on it one of these days."

~ ~ ~

Pam's backyard was mostly pool, but the grassy side area was large enough to hold the thirty guests. Pam stood in the doorway with her new boyfriend, one of the cameramen from the show. He must have been twenty years her junior. At first it didn't make sense to Sasha, but then she remembered that nothing made sense anymore. What was sense, anyway? She always lived life with the assumption that a higher order, not necessarily God but a universal truth, was in place. The past months had knocked that belief system out of orbit, and now Pam, a capable, independent, late-forties producer, had her hand in the back pocket of a rugged, quiet twentysomething. If you could let go of the way things *should be,* everything just *was*.

Suddenly Sasha's mom squeezed herself between Pam and the cameraman, another sight Sasha had never anticipated seeing. Her mom waved as she approached. "Love this house," she said, a mojito in hand. Seeing her parents in California was wild, the reason they were here wilder. Sasha took it all in: her mom and Jordan examining some flowers; Erika gesticulating to the caterer; Fritz arriving with his new girlfriend, who looked alarmingly like him.

Dr. Banks arrived in a flowing skirt and a white tank top, her smile as genuine and warm as it had been the day Sasha walked into her office six months earlier. Only the doctor, Jordan, Erika, and Sasha's parents knew the story behind the pregnancy, and their knowledge was reflected in winks and furtive glances. Everyone else thought Sasha and Jordan had slept together and she'd gotten pregnant by accident. Sasha was okay with this theory, as eventually they had.

Sasha grabbed her mom and ushered her over to meet Dr. Banks, and the two women stayed huddled together in conversation for most of the party. Later Sasha spotted her dad and the cameraman throwing a ball for Pam's basset hound, Digger, and reminded herself: it just *was*.

At lunch, talk turned to the unusual *Dateline* special that had finally aired the week before. "I thought it was a joke," Pam said, laughing. "Lazy sperm?" She turned to Dr. Banks. "You're a doctor. What gives?"

Sasha and Jordan were kicking each other under the table. Dr. Banks shrugged. "There are so many things we don't know about," she said. "That's the beauty of medicine. Anything's possible."

"Come on," Pam said. "I know about the birds and the bees. I've never heard anything about the lazy birds and the lazy bees." She looked toward Sasha. "Hey, maybe we can do a sketch about lazy birds and bees," she said, laughing. Thankfully, the conversation naturally moved to another subject.

Before dessert arrived, Erika clinked her glass for a toast.

"Sasha's been my best friend since we were five, and I'm genuinely honored to be part of her amazing, unpredictable life. How lucky to be her firstborn," she said, raising her glass. Everyone laughed and raised their glasses, too.

Sasha excused herself to go to the bathroom. She slipped past Digger, begging at her feet, and made her way inside Pam's house. She sat on the toilet, her belly resting on her legs. She wasn't huge, the way she'd seen other women carry. She was due in less than a month, and she imagined she'd grow substantially before then. It was hard to believe she was at her own baby shower. She said it out loud: "My baby shower."

When Sasha and Erika were kids, they attended a camp where archery was one of the activities. Much to her surprise, Sasha found that she loved the sport. She loved the precise movements of pulling back the bow, the resistance, and the challenge of hitting the right spot. There was pain involved—her elbow, her hand, even her ear—but it was all worth it when she heard that perfect *ping* as she released the arrow. Sometimes the arrow just fizzled to the ground, but the stronger she became, the better control she had, and that arrow flew. Over the past few months she'd felt like the bow, going back, back, back. But now, finally, she'd felt like the arrow, sailing forward into the future. She didn't know where she would land or how far she would travel, but she loved the feeling of being in midair.

"Sasha?" It was Jordan outside the door. Sasha flushed, quickly washed her hands, and opened the door. He stepped in before she could step out and started kissing her before she could ask what was happening. He had her pinned against the sink, his body dodging her belly. She could taste a tinge of tequila on his breath.

"I wanted to make a toast," he said.

"You should have."

"It would have been inappropriate," he said. "So I thought I'd make it to you in private."

"Okay." Sasha laughed.

Jordan found a cup and filled it with water. He took a quick sip and then held it high. "Up until now it's been about sex."

"Not really," Sasha said.

"Not done," Jordan said.

"Sorry."

"But from now on"—he raised the cup higher—"it's about love."

Sasha smiled and leaned into Jordan the way that kitten had leaned into her a few months ago. She rubbed her cheek against his. She whispered in his ear, "And some sex."

They stayed in the bathroom far longer than they should have, and when they rejoined the party Sasha looked around and saw what people call a community. And she would call on this community to help her with her child. And she would count on them because she knew that she could. The presents were piled, colorful and high, but none were as vibrant as her friends and family. She felt safe in the knowledge that a baby, her baby, despite all odds and circumstances, would arrive to this.

Acknowledgments

Kevin Salter suggested I write this story as a novel, and so I gave Sasha his last name.

The real Erika, best friend and doctor extraordinaire. She provided me with many medical terms and conditions and helped with the creation and credibility of this book.

I am beyond grateful to Howard Kaminsky for acting as my agent and guiding my novel into the right hands.

Thank you to Ann Campbell at Broadway Books for being the right hands. She is by far the best editor I could have hoped for. Thanks to Ursula Cary, Laura Lee Mattingly, Joanna Pinsker, and Julia Coblentz, too.

Thanks to my fantastic early-draft note givers: Miranda Banks, Jennifer Caloyeras, Ron and Sheila Clark, Bill Jacobson, Jennifer Kagan, David Rubenstein, and Rochelle Strauss. Special thanks to Les Plesko and the UCLA group.

Also, to Adam, Al, Basil, Daniela, Doug, Jessica, Jill, Joanne, John, Katie, Lara, Lisa, Liz, Mark, Max, Michelle, Mindy, Percy, Susan, and Suzan: thank you for all your support and encouragement while writing this book!

© ADAM DAVID MELTZER

about the author

MELISSA CLARK is the creator and executive producer of the award-winning television series *Braceface*, and has written for shows on the Cartoon Network, the Disney Channel, and FOX. She received a master's degree from the writing program at U.C. Davis, and currently lives in Los Angeles. This is her first novel.

www.swimmingupstreamslowly.com